Heart OF A Dolphin

Catherine Hapka

SCHOLASTIC INC.

ISBN 978-1-338-03282-6

10 9 8 7 6 5 4 3 2 1   16 17 18 19 20

Printed in the U.S.A.   40

First printing 2016

Book design by Mary Claire Cruz

Annie's Town

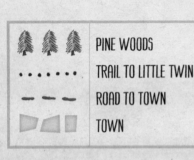

PINE WOODS	
····· TRAIL TO LITTLE TWIN	
‒ ‒ ‒ ROAD TO TOWN	
TOWN	

MR. REED'S
RESTAURANT

BEACH

LITTLE
TWIN

THE SPIT

THE MARINA

SHOPS

THE DOCKVIEW

SHOPS

TO
NEW
LONDON

TWIN COVES POINT

ANNIE'S HOUSE

BIG TWIN

EMMA'S HOUSE

LIGHTHOUSE LIBRARY

TO
NEW
HAVEN

BROOKE &
ZOE'S HOUSE

MORGAN'S HOUSE

LONG ISLAND
SOUND

1

It was my little brother Will's birthday, which meant the official start of summer. Oh, school had been out for two or three weeks already, and sunscreen-smeared tourists had been snarling traffic in our coastal Connecticut town even longer than that. But by Will's birthday, the water had warmed up enough that my toes didn't turn numb when I swam, and blackfish season was open again.

We were celebrating with a party and cookout on the half-sand, half-stone beach of Little Twin, the smaller of Twin Coves Point's coves. Mom was taking the whole day off for a change, and Jacob had

1

torn himself away from his college-prep stuff, and two kids from Will's class had actually showed up. Emma was there, too, of course. She always came to our family parties—she was pretty much an honorary Reed after being my best friend for as many of our eleven and a half years as either of us could remember.

"Where's Daddy? Where's Daddy? Where's Daddy?" Will chanted, sounding closer to three years old than to just-turning-eight. His blue eyes were wide and a little crazy-looking, probably because his birthday was the one day he was allowed to eat all the junk food he wanted.

Mom glanced up from her book, sweeping a strand of auburn hair off her forehead where the breeze had blown it. Her hair used to be the exact same color as mine and Will's—bright strawberry blond—but one day a few months ago, I'd noticed hers was starting to look different. When I'd grabbed a handful to take a closer look, I could see strands of silvery-gray all through it. A few days after that, Mom came home with a bag from the drugstore, and the next morning, her hair was darker all over.

"Daddy will be here in a little while, honey," Mom told Will now. Her eyes were tired and I could tell she was trying to sound patient, but it was hard to be patient when Will asked the same question a million times. I knew that better than anyone.

"Come here, Will," Jacob called from over near the tidal pool at the rocky end of the crescent-shaped beach. "I'm showing the guys how to skip stones. Don't you want to try?"

The other kids barely glanced at the birthday boy. They were arguing over a flat stone. Finally one of them, a pale kid with a turned-up nose, grabbed the stone and tossed it toward the water, where it landed with a plop and disappeared.

"Rats!" The kid sounded frustrated. "I can't get it."

The other kid grinned. "Maybe you need to chop off a couple fingers and you'll be better." His eyes wandered to my older brother's left hand, which was missing the pinky and ring fingers almost all the way to the lower knuckles. Jacob had lost those fingers in a boating accident when he was five, which was the year before I was born. He hardly seemed to miss them, and I'd never known him any other way, so I didn't notice it much either until someone started staring.

"Check it out, Annie." Emma poked me in the back.

I rolled over toward her, wiggling my hip to avoid a sharp stone that was poking me through my towel. "What?"

She pointed at the fashion magazine she'd been flipping through. "Do you think I could pull off this outfit?"

I wrinkled my nose. "Why would you want to? It looks like she's wearing a giant paper towel."

"Stop." Emma giggled and pointed to the opposite page. "Okay, what about this one?"

I sat up, tired of lying around. "Let's go body-surfing or something. Oh! Or we could snorkel—I found a really cool moon snail out there last week."

"Nah." Emma licked her finger and turned the page. "I want to work on my tan."

I stared at her, wondering if she was joking. She never used to care about stuff like tanning and fashion magazines. This was a different Emma, one I didn't understand.

She even *looked* different. I'd noticed it the first time I saw her in a swimsuit that summer. Over the winter, beneath all those layers of clothes, she'd changed. Parts of her had slimmed down, and other parts had filled out, and she was at least two inches taller than me now—not that that was saying much.

Anyway, I didn't like it. Things weren't supposed to change when I wasn't paying attention. Especially not best friends.

Trying not to think about that, I grabbed the magazine out of her hands. "Quit reading and talk to me, or I'll throw this in the water!" I warned playfully.

She squealed, trying to grab it back. "You better not—I spent the last of my allowance on that!"

I didn't answer. Emma's family was rich—*really* rich. Her mom was a famous painter, and her dad had been born into one of the richest families in New York City and then became a zillionaire all over again on his own. Their house was called the Cottage, but it was actually the largest of the four houses on Twin Coves Point. Of the remaining three houses, two of them were almost as big and fancy as the Cottage, only newer. The last house was where my family lived. It used to be a caretaker's cottage for one of the bigger houses until my mom's grandfather bought it a long time ago. We'd been there forever, which was the only reason we could afford to live anywhere near the Point, let alone on it.

Anyway, Emma could afford all the fashion magazines in Connecticut if she really wanted them. But her parents said they didn't want to spoil her, so they made her stick to an allowance, at least most of the time.

Emma leaned back on her elbows, her long, wavy brown hair brushing against her towel. It was almost as long as mine now, and I was surprised she hadn't made me measure it lately. We used to do that all the time back when we both first started growing it out.

"When's your dad getting here, anyway? I'm starving," Emma said.

"He promised to come as soon as the lunch rush was over." I could only hope he actually made it, or Will was going to freak out.

My dad was a chef. Up until the previous fall, he'd worked at this famous restaurant right by the harbor called the Dockview, which had been in business for over a hundred years. Then his uncle died and left him some money, and Dad decided to open his own restaurant, Mike's Seafood. Apparently it was his lifelong dream, even though he'd never said a peep to me about it.

Ever since, he worked all the time. I mean, *all* the time. Every summer before this one, Dad and Jacob and I had gone fishing at least two or three times a week from the start of blue crab season until it got too cold in the fall. This year? We'd only been out on the boat a total of three times so far. And even those times weren't the same, since Dad had traded in our nice old fishing boat for a smaller, much less fancy one. He'd sold our sailboat, too. Raising capital, he'd called it, which sounded like something Emma's father would say.

"So when do you think the new people will move in?" Emma asked.

I was used to her sudden changes of subject. Her attention span was almost as short as Will's, though most people didn't seem to mind it as much coming from her.

"You mean Brooke's house?" I asked, though I already knew the answer. Brooke was a year older than us. Her family had lived on the Point until they'd moved to Los Angeles at the end of the school year.

"Yeah." Emma's gaze wandered up the steep wall of the cove, though all we could see from the beach was the schooner-shaped copper weather vane on the very tip-top of her own house. "Morgan heard the new family has a kid our age."

"Really?" I wanted to ask why she'd been talking to Morgan—again—but I bit my tongue. "Wow, it's kind of crazy that there always ends up being a girl around our age living in each house on the Point," I said instead.

"I know, right?" Emma squinted up at me. "But we don't know if it's a girl or a boy this time." She giggled. "Morgan hopes it's a boy."

"Yeah, she would," I muttered. Morgan Pierce had lived in the house between Emma's and Brooke's for years, but up until that summer, she'd thought she was too good to hang out with Emma and me. Maybe it was because her mom was on TV, or because her dad was a retired navy admiral from an old New England family that owned half of Connecticut. Or maybe she was just a natural-born snob.

Either way, Brooke moving away had left Morgan without a best friend, or anyone on the Point to hang out with at all. She was still totally ignoring me, but she'd started being a little friendlier to Emma. That was weird enough, but the even weirder thing? Emma didn't seem to mind all that much.

Over by the tidal pool, Will's friends were getting tired of skipping stones. "Let's go swimming," one of them said.

"Yeah!" Will charged toward the water.

"Will, wait," my mom's voice rang out, echoing off the high, rocky walls of the cove. "Aren't you forgetting something?"

"Huh? Oh." Will glanced at the bright red life jacket in Mom's hand, and his face fell. He slunk over and slipped it on.

One of the other boys laughed. "What're you doing?"

"Just in case," Will told him. That was what my parents always said: Just in case.

Will couldn't swim—not very well, anyway. Whenever his head went underwater, even in the pool-calm water of our little cove, he panicked and started flailing around and eventually sank. Which was weird, since the whole rest of the family was practically part fish. I learned to swim before I could really even walk—we had home movies that proved it. And I'd made the varsity swim team at my middle school right away, even though most people stayed on JV for at least a year.

"Come on, let's go in, too." I poked Emma on the shoulder.

"Ow." She swatted my finger away. "You go. It's still too cold for me."

"Fine." Her eyes were closed now, so she didn't see my frown. The old Emma loved to swim. I quickly wrapped my waist-length braid into a messy bun and secured it with an elastic. Then I headed for the water.

The younger boys were already splashing around in the shallows, throwing sand and trying to scare one another by pretending to see jellyfish and sharks every five seconds. It was a still day and the waves weren't big enough for bodysurfing, so I waded to the drop-off thirty feet out, where the water suddenly gets deep.

I'd forgotten my snorkeling mask and didn't feel like going back to get it. So I just dove down and skimmed along with my eyes closed, enjoying the feel of the cool water on my skin. When I came up for air, I heard splashing behind me and opened my eyes quickly, wondering if Emma had changed her mind about swimming.

It wasn't Emma, though. Jacob was bobbing in the water, grinning at me. His hair, dark and curly like Dad's, was plastered to his forehead.

"Want to race?" he asked. "Out to the spit and back."

"You're on."

I let myself sink under and did a strong whip kick, gliding forward before he had a chance to get moving. Then I surfaced and went straight into a front crawl, my arms windmilling steadily as if I was in the finals at a swim meet.

Suddenly I felt a hand grab my ankle. A sharp yank pulled me under, and I came up sputtering. "Cheater!" I yelled as my brother swam past me with a laugh.

I was about to lunge forward and dunk him, but he'd paused and shaded his face to stare at something. "What's that?" he said.

I followed his gaze and saw movement on the rocky spit at the edge of the cove. For a second, I panicked, thinking Will must have walked out there again. A lot of trash washed up on the spit, carried in from the harbor by the tides and trapped by the jagged rocks. One day last summer, Will had spotted a cool-looking bottle or something through Dad's binoculars and decided he wanted to retrieve it. So he'd waited until Jacob wasn't looking and sneaked off, picking his way along the precarious wall of stone and barnacles and algae. It was a miracle he hadn't slipped and fallen in and been swept all the way out to Long Island Sound. He'd ended up with a big gash on his foot from a piece of broken glass, though, and Jacob had been in big trouble for not paying enough attention when he was supposed to be watching him.

But a quick glance over my shoulder told me that Will was still splashing around safely in the shallows. I swam past Jacob, squinting against the sunlight glinting off the water. Blinking moisture out of my eyes, I saw a silvery shape huddled against the rocks.

"I think—I think it's a dolphin!" I exclaimed. "A bottlenose."

I stared in wonder. The sleek gray creature was pressed up against the rocks, half-submerged in the frothy little waves breaking against the spit. He looked just like the dolphins I'd seen many times at the aquarium over in Mystic. Or from the boat, where we occasionally spotted them swimming along in the distance, especially out toward the eastern end of the Sound.

Except this one was right here, less than ten feet in front of me. "Careful." Jacob was still treading water behind me. "It may look cute, but it's a wild animal. Don't get too close."

"I won't." I kicked forward a little more. "Why isn't he swimming away?"

"Annie, stop." Jacob sounded worried.

I ignored him, my gaze fixed on the dolphin. He wiggled and his tail slapped against the rock, but he stayed where he was.

"Easy, buddy," I said soothingly. "I'm not going to hurt you, I promise. I just want to see . . ."

My voice trailed off as the dolphin thrashed again, giving me a better look at the rest of his body.

"Oh gosh!" I glanced back at Jacob. "He's all tangled up in fishing line!" My heart pounded as I swam even closer, trying to get a better look. A tangle of what looked like heavy-duty braided line was wrapped around the dolphin's midsection and part of his tail, pretty much lashing him to the rocks behind him.

The dolphin stopped struggling for a moment, staring at me with dark eyes that were wise, gentle, and curious. There was a large, half-healed wound zigzagging across his face, starting in front of one eye and ending just short of the blowhole atop his head.

"Easy, easy," I murmured, using an eggbeater kick to steady myself as the current carried me toward the dolphin. "I'm your friend, okay?"

The dolphin let out a funny little chirping sound, but he stayed still as I tentatively reached toward him. I was vaguely aware of Jacob calling out to me again, but I barely heard him. I couldn't take my eyes off the dolphin. I'd never seen one up so close like this, not without a thick pane of glass between us, anyway. The dolphin seemed bigger than I would have expected, and maybe a little wilder, too. Somehow, though, I didn't really feel afraid, just weirdly shy. Holding my breath, I leaned forward and touched the dolphin's side.

His skin felt rubbery and smooth. I stroked it gently, and the dolphin chirped again, his gaze never leaving my face. I couldn't believe he was letting me pet him; it made me feel honored and sort of breathless, like the first time Emma's mom asked my opinion on one of her paintings. As I ran my hand up toward his dorsal fin, an extra-large wave washed past me, splashing up and making the dolphin thrash once more. I winced as the line dug deeper into that smooth gray skin.

I turned to see Jacob still bobbing in the water twenty yards back. "He's really stuck," I called. "The tide's coming in, and soon he won't be able to keep his blowhole above the surface. He'll die if we don't help him!"

2

The dolphin stopped struggling and stared at me, his eyes wary but curious at the same time.

"Hold on, buddy." I tried to sound soothing, though my voice shook a little. "I'm going to help you, okay?" I bit my lip, treading water and wishing my dad was there. He was good with animals, and he always knew what to do.

"Are you sure it's totally stuck?" Jacob called.

The dolphin started fighting the lines again, his tail and nose smacking against the hard rock. Glancing back, I saw Jacob dog-paddling toward me.

"Stop! Back off, okay?" I called. "I think he's scared of you."

"Okay. But be careful." Jacob swung his arms back, pulling himself through the water in a modified backstroke without taking his eyes off me.

I turned back toward the dolphin. He'd stopped banging against the rocks, though he still looked nervous.

"It's okay," I told him. "It's just us now."

The dolphin let out a soft chirp. I chirped back, doing my best to imitate the sound. Then I kicked forward a little, once again reaching toward him.

He didn't move, other than his eyes, which continued to watch me. I slid my hand toward the fishing line encircling his middle. It was so tight I couldn't even get a finger under it. When I tried, I heard the wet slap of the dolphin's tail hitting the sharp rocks.

Ouch. He didn't have to say it in people language for me to understand. I pulled my hand away.

"Wow, you're really wrapped up tight," I murmured, my heart jumping around like a frog in a bottle as I tried to figure out what to do. That line was good and strong—probably strong enough to land a hundred-pound cod.

"You'll need to cut it," Jacob called.

At the sound of his voice, the dolphin smacked the rocks with his tail again, letting out a loud squeak. I turned, shading my eyes to squint at my brother.

"What?" I said.

"A knife." He gestured toward the beach. "My multi-tool is in my bag. Let's go get it and make a plan."

"Let's make a plan" was one of Jacob's favorite phrases, and I almost smiled. But when a slightly bigger wave splashed up onto the wall of rocks, spraying me with briny foam, all I could think of was the tide, relentless and rising. We didn't have much time.

"Okay." I spit out a mouthful of salt water, then

glanced at the dolphin. "Be right back, buddy. Promise."

The dolphin let out a whistle as I kicked away from him, but I didn't look back. Instead I dove under the water, swimming after Jacob as fast as I could.

Back on the beach, Emma had finally lost interest in her magazine. She was standing with her toes in the water and one hand on her hip, watching the younger boys chase one another around nearby.

"What were you doing out there?" she asked, splashing toward me as I churned my way through the shallows.

"We found a dolphin," I said.

Her eyes widened. "A dolphin, here? Cool!"

"Not really," Jacob said. He was already digging into the old army-green backpack he carried everywhere. "It's trapped in some fishing line."

Mom had been unpacking the picnic hamper, but she stopped and looked over at me. "Really?"

"Uh-huh. He's all tied up," I told her. "He won't let Jacob come close—just me. If I don't get him loose, he'll drown!"

I guess I sounded pretty worked up, because even Will and his friends were coming over by then to find out what was going on. One of the boys laughed. "How can a fish drown?" he exclaimed.

"A dolphin's not a fish; it's a mammal," the other kid said. "Duh. If you weren't from dumb old New York City, you'd know that."

"Yeah!" Will cried, dancing around and almost tripping over his own feet. "Dumb York City! New Dumb City!"

"Shut up!" the other kid said heatedly. "The city beats this stupid hick place any day."

The three boys continued squabbling, but I stopped paying attention. "Hurry, Jacob." As I leaned over him, my dripping hair left wet dark spots on the dull green canvas backpack. "The tide's coming in fast. We have to get him loose."

Mom peered out toward the spit, then grabbed Will by the shoulder and started expertly unfastening the straps of his life jacket.

"Take this, Annie," she said. "If you're going back out there, you need to be safe."

I opened my mouth to argue. I couldn't remember the last time I'd worn a life jacket in our quiet little cove. Wait—yes I could. It was last summer when we'd been fishing nearby and Dad had decided to bring the boat in to surprise Mom and Will on the beach. But that was different. I always wore a life jacket when we were out on the boat. That was the rule. But swimming? No way, not even in the harbor, let alone the cove.

At Mom's look, I closed my mouth without saying a word. "Okay, thanks," I said, slipping my arms through the holes and buckling the straps. Maybe she was right. It would be easier to work on those lines if I didn't have to worry about keeping myself afloat.

Jacob finally found the multi-tool. He handed it

to me. "Try the scissors first," he said, flipping open one of the tools to show me. "If they're not strong enough, the wire cutters should do the trick." He closed the tool up again and tucked it into the zipper pocket of his trunks. "Come on— I'll swim out most of the way with you."

"Should I come, too?" Emma asked.

"That's okay," I told her. "The dolphin might get scared if too many people go."

"Oh. Okay." She looked a little disappointed, and I almost said she could come anyway. Then I remembered the tide creeping up those rocks and kept quiet. Emma probably didn't want to swim all the way out there anyway. She was just trying to be a good friend. But right now, the most important thing was saving the dolphin. I had to focus on that.

Jacob was already splashing back out through the shallows. I followed, checking to make sure my bun hadn't come loose. I loved having long hair, but sometimes it could get in the way a little, especially when it was wet.

"Good luck, Annie!" Emma called.

Lifting a hand to show I'd heard her, I took a deep breath and dove into a small oncoming wave.

I caught up to my brother a short distance from the spit. Gulping in air, I glanced ahead at the dolphin. The water had already risen another couple of inches.

"Here." Jacob handed me the tool and gave me a small smile. "Try not to drop it, okay?"

The dolphin flopped around a little when I came closer. "It's okay—it's just me," I said. "I'm here to help."

My voice only made him thrash harder. Oh no! What if he'd decided to be scared of me now, too? What if I couldn't get close enough to cut him free?

"Easy, easy," I singsonged, feeling a little desperate. Maybe I should let Jacob try; he was stronger . . .

Suddenly I had another idea. Taking a breath, I imitated the dolphin's chirp the way I had earlier.

His thrashing slowed, then stopped. I stayed quiet for a moment, waiting. He stared at me—and let out a questioning squeak.

I squeaked back, once again doing my best to imitate him, and finally the dolphin relaxed. I smiled with relief, wondering what I'd just said to him in dolphin language. Probably nothing, but it didn't matter. Just hearing a familiar sound must have been enough.

"Hold still, okay?" I said in people language. "I'm going to cut you loose. You can trust me. I promise."

This time the dolphin didn't panic when I swam closer. He flinched slightly but otherwise stayed still as I carefully slid the bottom blade of the scissors under the closest bit of line. Doing my best not to cut him, I squeezed the handle. It caught and stopped, and when I squeezed harder, the tool bucked in my hand like a fish at the end of a line. I scrabbled to hold on to it, poking my thumb on the end of the scissors in the process. But I barely noticed the pain, breathing a sigh of relief that I hadn't dropped the tool.

"Everything okay over there?" Jacob called, still treading water where I'd left him.

"Fine," I called back. Then I smiled at the dolphin. "Okay, let's try the wire snips."

The water this far out was still a little chilly this time of year, and my hands felt clumsy-numb and slippery as I fumbled with the tool. But finally I found the right blade and snapped it open.

This time the dolphin squeaked and wiggled when I reached for him. I let out a few more chirps and then just murmured soothingly, not even sure what I was saying. But when I looked in the creature's eyes, I could tell he was listening, and I smiled again. He trusted me; I could feel it. I couldn't let him down.

I held my breath as I slid the new blade into place. *Please let it work please let it work . . .* The air whooshed out of me with relief as the line gave way immediately.

"Got it!" I yelled to Jacob.

My call startled the dolphin, and he burst into motion. The front part of his body had come partway loose with the cutting of the line, and I cried out in dismay as he thrashed, afraid he'd really hurt himself against the rocks.

The dolphin stopped moving suddenly, turning his head to stare at me. Had he understood my cry? I held my breath as our eyes locked, and it was as if he was reading my mind—or maybe my heart. We stayed like that until a wave splashed up onto my chin, reminding me that I had to hurry.

"Good boy," I whispered. "That's right. Just let me get the rest of the lines . . ."

I went back to work, carefully snipping one piece of line after another. Some of them had already cut into his skin a little, and I hoped they wouldn't leave a mark.

That reminded me of the scar running down the dolphin's face. Glancing at it out of the corner of my eye as I worked, I wondered what had caused it. Had he tangled with a shark, or run into a boat's propeller? Was that scar maybe the reason the dolphin seemed to be all alone in the cove, with no pod in sight?

I forgot all that as the last bit of line gave way. "There!" I exclaimed, using the hand that wasn't holding the tool to push back from the rocky spit. If the dolphin leaped away from the rocks, I didn't want to be in his way. He might not be full grown, but he still outweighed me by at least a hundred pounds.

But the dolphin barely moved, floating there between me and the spit. His tail end sank down out of sight, but his head stayed above water, his dark eyes still watching me.

"You can go now," I told him softly. "You're free."

The dolphin let out a funny little whistle. Then he moved forward, bumping me gently with his snout.

I smiled, carefully reaching out to stroke his head. My fingers lingered near that old scar, tracing it down his face. He stayed perfectly still, emitting several tiny chirps.

"You're welcome," I whispered.

"Did you get it, Annie?"

At the sound of Jacob's voice, the dolphin burst into motion, disappearing beneath the waves with a flip of his tail. I squinted at the spot, hoping he'd resurface. But he was gone. I was a little disappointed, but mostly relieved that our plan had worked.

"Got it," I called back to my brother, flipping the multi-tool shut. "He's free."

I was still smiling when my foot touched the gritty sand of the shallows a few minutes later. "We saw it!" Will bellowed, racing forward to meet me. "You saved it, Annie!"

"Yeah." I wasn't sure what else to say as I glanced around at the others. Everyone looked excited and a little awed, even though nobody except Will said anything for a second—not even Emma, who almost always had a lot to say.

"I'm proud of you, Annie," Mom said at last. "I wish your dad had been here—or at least that I'd thought to take some pictures. It's not often you see dolphins in the harbor, let alone right here in our cove!"

"I know, right?" Emma laughed. "Leave it to Annie to find one!"

I shrugged off the life jacket, handing it back to Will. "Actually, Jacob saw him first."

"But Annie saved him," Jacob said. "That dolphin wasn't about to let me anywhere near him. Guess he liked you better, little sis."

"Guess so." I smiled at him. Even though his tone was light, I could tell he'd sensed it, too. That special moment between me and the dolphin. I'd never felt anything like it before.

"That dolphin owes you, Annie," Emma said with a grin. "The least he could do is come back and give us rides or something. Wouldn't that be cool?"

Will hooted with laughter and clapped his hands. "Yeah! Like a dolphin Jet Ski!"

I rolled my eyes. Will was obsessed with Jet Skis. He might have the world's shortest attention span, but he could spend hours at the marina watching people zoom in and out on the noisy machines. With a loud *vroom, vroom!* he started running around in circles, kicking up sand with each step.

I frowned, wishing Will could be . . . well, not so *Will* all the time. But whatever. It was his birthday, and I didn't want to get annoyed with him if I could help it.

"I think I know why the dolphin liked me," I told everyone. "I talked to him in his own language."

That stopped Will short. "You speak dolphin language?" he exclaimed. "No way!"

"Yeah, no way!" one of his friends echoed.

I smiled. "Just listen . . ."

The boys looked impressed as I let out a series of chirps and whistles. Mom chuckled.

"Very good, Annie," she said. "Your dad always says you're half fish. Maybe you're actually half dolphin."

Emma giggled. "Maybe we should start calling her Squeak."

"Or maybe we should call her dolphin that," Jacob said.

"Yeah." One of the younger boys glanced out into the cove. "Do you think Squeak'll come back?"

"No way," his friend said. "Besides, how could we even tell it was him? All dolphins look the same."

"Not this one," I told him. "He's got a big scar zigzagging right across his face, like this." I demonstrated on my own face.

"Really?" Will giggled. "Maybe we should call him Admiral Squeak!"

That made all of us laugh except for Mom, who tsk-tsked quietly, though I was pretty sure she was holding back a smile. Morgan's father, Admiral Ezekiel Pierce, was known around town as Admiral Zeke. His navy career had left him with a distinctive and rather distinguished scar across one cheek, which now that I thought about it, did look a little like the one on the dolphin's face.

Just then, I caught a flash of movement halfway down the steep, narrow pathway leading into the cove from the houses above. I gulped as I recognized the figure's blond pixie cut and freckled arms.

"Shh," I warned, elbowing Emma. "Here comes Morgan."

Morgan didn't have much of a sense of humor as far as I could tell, especially about herself and her family, and she always seemed to be looking for reasons to get mad at people. I doubted she'd be amused by Will's nickname for the scar-faced dolphin. And the last thing poor Will needed was to make an enemy of Morgan Pierce.

"Promise you won't say anything about the dolphin, okay?" I whispered to my family and Emma. "I don't want her to figure out why we were laughing."

"But—" Will began.

I grabbed his shoulder and squeezed it. "Just do it, okay?" I said. "I'll buy you an ice cream later. Double scoop for your birthday."

By then Morgan had reached the bottom of the path and started picking her way gingerly across the sharp stones. She was barefoot, dressed in a swimsuit and a pair of cut-offs.

"Hi, Morgan!" Emma called out. "What's up?"

"Nothing much." Morgan sounded bored. "What are you guys doing here?"

Her grayish-blue eyes swept over all of us, lingering on Will, who was dancing around with a goofy expression on his face—probably already trying to figure out which two of the local ice cream shop's forty-three flavors he'd get.

"It's Will's birthday, Morgan," Mom said. "We're going to have a picnic as soon as Mike gets here. Would you like to join us?"

I winced. Everyone on the Point knew that Morgan liked me about as much as a sea urchin spine to the foot—and that she liked Will even less. How could Mom invite her to our family party?

"Thanks, Mrs. Reed," Morgan said in the sickly sweet talking-to-adults voice that seemed to convince most of the town that she was a nice person. "But I already ate lunch. Actually, I just came to find Emma and see if she wants to come swimming in my pool."

"Oh! Um . . ." Emma shot me an anxious look. Probably trying to figure out how to turn down Morgan's invitation politely, I figured.

Morgan followed her gaze. "Oh yeah, you're invited, too, Annie," she added. "If you want."

She couldn't have sounded less enthusiastic if she'd tried. I forced a smile.

"Thanks, but I can't," I said. "Like Mom said, we're right in the middle of Will's party."

"Okay." Morgan turned away. "Coming, Ems?"

Emma shot me another uncertain glance. "Um, sure, a swim sounds great," she said. "You guys don't mind if I take off, right? I'm actually not that hungry anyway."

My jaw dropped in shock as she grabbed her stuff and followed Morgan up the path without a backward glance. What in the world had happened to my best friend?

Jacob didn't give me much time to think about it. "Tag—you're it!" he said, poking me in the shoulder and taking off for the shallows.

"Not for long!" I shouted back, leaping after him. It was bad enough that Emma had suddenly gone crazy—I didn't want anyone to see how much it bugged me. "Come on, Will. Let's get him!"

3

Two days later, I was wiping down one of the tables near the restaurant's big front window, mostly ignoring the mobs of tourists wandering around outside. This side of the harbor wasn't quite as busy as the other side, where the marina and the Dockview and most of the souvenir shops were, but it was busy enough. Almost half the restaurant's tables were full, which was pretty good for two o'clock on a Sunday.

Then I noticed a woman strolling by with a pair of trim little terriers tugging at the ends of their leashes. Straightening up and dropping my rag back in my apron pocket, I smiled as the dogs turned and pounced on a blowing leaf. I'd always wanted a dog, but Will was allergic to everything with fur. We'd even had to send our cat over to live with Emma when Mom and Dad had realized she was the reason baby Will always had itchy eyes and hives. I'd been able to visit her whenever I wanted, of course, and Emma had taken good care of her until she'd died of old age two years ago. But it still bugged me a little when I thought about it.

Too bad Admiral Squeak can't be my pet, I thought as I ran my rag over the table.

The silly name had stuck in my head, but it didn't stop me from still feeling awed and wistful whenever I thought about the dolphin—I'd never forget the way he had looked at me, the way he'd trusted me to set him free. More than anything, I wished I could see him again.

Dolphins aren't furry, I told myself with a smile. *So maybe Will wouldn't be allergic to him. Admiral*

Squeak could live in the bathtub, and I could exercise him in the cove on a special leash . . .

Suddenly I noticed a customer waving her napkin at me. "Over here, honey," she called in a thick Boston accent. "I'm all out of iced tea."

She waved a hand full of glittery rings at her empty glass. Her companion, a skinny man in Bermuda shorts and a bow tie, grabbed his own glass and downed it in one gulp.

" 'Nother cold one for me, too," he said, slamming the glass down on the table so hard it made me jump.

I smiled weakly at the pair, then glanced around for the waitress, a college student named Crystal who liked to duck into the bathroom to play with her phone every half hour or so. Dad had muttered about firing her more than once, but so far she was the only server he'd found who was willing to work brunch shift on weekends, so she stayed.

"Um, okay," I told the customers. "Someone will be right out with that."

I zigzagged my way through the maze of tables and pushed through the swinging door into the kitchen. As usual, it was hot and steamy in there, smelling of fish and black pepper. Dad glanced up from the stove, where he was stirring something in an enormous stainless steel pot.

"Everything okay out front, Snappy?" he asked, grabbing a rag to mop his brow. Snappy was his favorite nickname for me. I'd earned it at age five when I'd brought home a snapping turtle I'd found, setting it free in the living room, where it promptly bit Mom on the toe.

I told him about the Boston couple's drink order. He frowned.

"Where's Crystal?" he asked.

At that moment, Mom came in from the pantry carrying a bushel of sweet corn. Dad told her what was going on, and she sighed.

"I'll get the drinks," she said. "After that I'll find Crystal and remind her that she's supposed to be working for a living."

"Don't be too hard on her, Suz," Dad said. "Nobody's even responded to this week's ad. Guess all the college kids already found summer jobs."

"Or decided they'd rather play than work." Mom sounded a little grumpy.

I couldn't blame her. She had a full-time job as a nurse at a medical practice out on the highway. As soon as she got off, she usually headed straight for the restaurant, where she put in another few hours helping with the dinner shift. On weekends, she was there pretty much all day right alongside Dad.

After she'd hurried out, Dad tasted the contents of the pot, then held out the spoon to me. "What do you think, Snappy?"

I blew on the steaming liquid and sucked it down. The broth was garlicky and rich and tasted of tomato and spicy sausage and the sea. It was so hot it burned my throat going down, but it was worth it.

"Delicious," I told him with a smile. "Like always."

"Hmm." Dad grabbed a clean spoon for another taste before tossing both spoons in the sink. "Could use a little more salt, I think."

He added a generous pinch, then threw in a few more herbs and spices for good measure, looking kind of like a mad scientist as he stirred it all together. His seafood stew was already becoming famous among some of the locals, including the Portuguese fishermen who came every day for early supper after bringing in their catches. Somehow, though, the tourists didn't seem to be getting the message. They still flocked to the Dockview every night, sometimes snaking out the door and halfway down the block as they waited for a table.

I picked up the spoons Dad had dropped in the sink, washing them along with several other dishes already in there. Just as I finished, he stepped away from the bubbling pot, seeming satisfied. He wiped his hands on his apron and studied my face.

"You look thoughtful, Annie," he said. "What's eating you?"

"Nothing," I said. Then I shrugged. "Just thinking about that dolphin, I guess."

"Admiral Squeak?" He smiled. "Yeah, still wish I'd been there to see that. But I'm proud of you for helping that poor creature, Annie."

"I had to." My mind wandered back to the way the dolphin had met my gaze, his eyes wise and curious. "It was like . . ." I hesitated, shooting him a sidelong look, wondering if he'd think I was crazy. "Like we were friends, or had a bond, or something. Like we were, you know, communicating. Heart to heart, or something."

Dad nodded, looking thoughtful. "Sometimes that happens," he says. "With animals, and with people, too. Like when your mom and I first met." He winked. "Actually, I felt the bond instantly. It took her a couple of months and a whole lot of flowers and fancy dinners before she felt it, too."

It was a familiar joke, but it still made me smile. "Anyway, I wish I knew he was okay," I said, twisting the dishrag between my hands. "Squeak, I mean. What if his cuts got infected or something? Or what if his pod abandoned him when he got tangled up and he can't find them again?"

"Maybe we should go out in the boat tomorrow and look around," Dad suggested. "See if we can find the admiral and maybe the rest of his pod. What do you say?"

"Sure, that'd be cool." I felt a flicker of interest, though I tried not to get my hopes up. The restaurant was closed on Mondays, and Dad was always suggesting excursions and activities to fill his one day off. Somehow, though, there always seemed to be some business he had to take care of instead, like going to the bank or over to the fish market or all the way into New Haven to get some piece of equipment fixed.

Just then, Mom hurried back into the kitchen with Crystal at her heels. "Is the omelet done yet?"

Crystal asked Dad. "The guy decided he doesn't want mushrooms in it after all."

Dad grimaced, glancing at the pan on the next burner, where an omelet was sizzling. "No problem," he said. "I'll fire another one."

As he grabbed eggs from the cooler and Crystal disappeared back into the dining room, Mom started stacking clean water glasses on a tray.

"Annie," she said, "we're almost out of change out front—I need you to run to the ATM and withdraw some tens, then stop and ask Mr. Booth if he can spare us some change."

"Okay." My heart sank. I didn't mind the ATM trip, but Mr. Booth was a cranky old coot who'd been running our town's busy bike rental place since the oceans were formed. At least that was what Emma's dad always said.

I pulled off my apron and tossed it on the hook by the pantry. Then I ducked out the back door, not wanting to chance being stopped by demanding customers.

As I emerged from the narrow alley between the restaurant and the bookshop next door, I almost collided with Emma. "Oh!" she blurted out. "Annie. What are you doing here?"

I told her about my errand. "Want to come?' I asked, glad that she'd turned up for a visit at just the right moment. Everyone in town adored friendly, outgoing Emma—even Mr. Booth. "We can have clam strips when we get back," I told her with a smile. "Dad just made a fresh batch."

"Um . . ." Her hazel eyes darted around, not quite meeting my gaze. "Actually, I can't."

"What do you mean?" I reached into the pocket of my shorts, checking that Dad's bank card was still there. "It'll only take a sec."

"It's not that. I was just on my way somewhere, and, um . . ."

At that moment, I heard someone call Emma's name. I tensed, recognizing the voice instantly.

When I turned to look, Morgan was strolling toward us. Right behind her were the Sullivan triplets, Samantha, Sophia, and Sydney, who were Brooke's age and lived in one of the new McMansions out near the highway, which made them regular-rich rather than rich-rich like Morgan and Emma. Grace Ogawa was there, too. She was the only Asian kid in our class, and seemed to think she was some kind of celebrity because she and her younger brother, Mattie, had been in the newspaper last summer for finding a tourist's lost dog. It turned out the tourist was some semi-famous Broadway actor, and thanks to Morgan's mom, the story had been mentioned on the national prime-time news show where she was one of the anchors.

"Great," I muttered to Emma out of the corner of my mouth. "The whole gang's here."

"Shh," Emma hissed. "They'll hear you."

I blinked at her. Since when did she care what Morgan and her friends thought of us?

But Emma wasn't looking at me. She was smiling and stepping forward to meet the other girls.

"Hey!" she said. "Sorry I'm late—my mom made me look at one of her dumb paintings on my way past."

"Oh." Morgan's gaze swept over me. "I thought maybe you decided to go wash dishes at the local crab shack." She glanced over at the restaurant with a smirk, and I frowned.

"Yeah right," Sophia piped up with a giggle. "Like even Cinder Emma would want to do that instead of hanging out with us!"

Cinder Emma? That was a new one. I shot another look at my best friend, waiting for her to react—maybe even punch Sophia in the nose like she'd done to Bertie Bickle back in second grade when he'd decided to nickname her Empty.

But if anything, Emma's smile just got bigger. For the first time, I noticed she was wearing makeup—tinted lip gloss and something sparkly on her eyelids. Her board shorts looked brand-new, too, and the straps of her flip-flops were lined with little jewels.

My gaze shifted to the other girls' feet. Sydney and Grace were both wearing the exact same flip-flops as Emma's, only with different colored jewels. Weird.

"Let's go already," Morgan said. "It smells around here." She cast another disdainful look toward the restaurant, and my cheeks went hot.

Samantha giggled uncertainly, her big brown eyes skittering over my face and then settling on the harbor, which looked still and glassy under the midday summer sun. "Yeah," she said. "Anyway, Connor and the guys might not wait for us if we're late."

"Yes they will." Morgan sounded confident. "But still, let's get moving."

Connor? Samantha had to be talking about her cousin, who was thirteen and totally obnoxious. He'd made Will cry once by stealing his socks. Who does that to a little kid? Creepy Connor Sullivan, that's who.

"Come on, Cinder Emma," Grace sang out

before turning and hurrying off down the sidewalk. "You'll love Jet Skiing!"

"Jet Skiing?" I echoed as Morgan and the triplets took off, too, not even looking back to see if Emma was following. "Since when do you like Jet Skiing?"

She shrugged, looking a little distracted. "Oh, you know me," she said, squinting after the other girls. "I'll try anything once."

That wasn't true at all. There was a long list of things Emma had always avoided, like eating eggplant and touching toads with her bare hands. Near the top of the list was Jet Skiing—she'd always been scared of trying it, even though I'd done it a couple of times with one of Jacob's old girlfriends.

She grabbed my hand and squeezed it. "I'll call you later, okay? Maybe we can plan our first beach sleepover of the season, right?"

That made me feel better, at least a little. Emma's artist mother had come up with the beach sleepover idea years ago. First we'd pour vast quantities of sand over the wide wooden floor-boards of the Cottage's huge old front porch, then Emma and I would decorate the railings with pretty shells and stones and twining bits of sea-weed, and spend the night out there in side by side hammocks. It was like camping on the beach, but much more comfortable. And I loved letting the waves lull me off to sleep. They sounded so close out there—much closer than the distant mumble I could hear from my little bedroom back in the scrub pines.

Emma squeezed my hand once more, then dropped it. "See you," she said quickly, dashing off after the other girls.

I watched her catch up and bump Grace with her shoulder. Then I turned away, focusing on what she'd just said about the beach sleepover. Emma might be changing, but some things always stayed the same.

"Best friends forever," I murmured as I set off toward the ATM.

4

On Tuesday morning, I was awakened by the harsh squawk of a gull right outside my window. Yawning and stretching as I sat up, I glanced at the clock on the bedside table. It was past nine o'clock. The gull called again and then went silent.

My house was silent as well. When I went downstairs, the kitchen smelled like stale coffee and there was a pile of dishes in the sink. A note on the fridge flapped in the breeze whispering in through the screens.

A: Took W. with me. J. is in his room. Love, Dad

I poured myself a glass of juice and headed up the rickety stairs to Jacob's tiny room under the eaves. But it was just as silent and empty as the rest of the house.

That was typical lately. Jacob was probably the most responsible seventeen-year-old in Connecticut, which was why my parents had been letting him babysit Will and me since he was my age. Now that he was almost a senior, though, he was obsessed with getting into a good college—and especially with getting lots of scholarships to help pay for it. He wanted to get a degree in accounting so he could come back to help Dad run the restaurant. I just hoped the restaurant was still in business by then, or Jacob might have to figure out a new plan. Anyway, I figured he'd probably forgotten all about me and headed off to the library or something.

By the time I got back downstairs, I'd drained my juice. Setting the glass in the sink, I stepped out the back door and took in a deep breath of warm, humid, sea-scented air. Birds flitted around in the scratchy branches of the pines all around the house, and a squirrel was digging busily for something in the sandy ground nearby.

I felt at loose ends. Glancing toward the road leading off through the trees in the direction of town, I thought about walking or biking down to the restaurant to help out. Instead, though, I turned the opposite way, heading for the steep trail down to Little Twin.

By the time I reached the beach, I was already sweating. The breeze had died down to almost nothing, which meant the water in the cove was even calmer than normal. I peeled off my shorts— as usual I had my swimsuit on underneath—and waded out a little way, sitting down and letting the tiny waves lap against me up to my elbows.

Staring out over the cove, I couldn't help think-ing how strange this summer was turning out to be. Yesterday's trip out in the boat to look for Admiral Squeak hadn't happened, just as I'd predicted. One of the burners on the stove was clogged, and there was some kind of problem with that week's oyster delivery, and by the time all that was taken care of, it was almost dinnertime.

Then there was Emma. She hadn't called on Sunday, or most of Monday. I'd finally wandered over and found her helping her dad and the gardener prune the rosebushes, but she hadn't mentioned the beach sleepover at all, and for some reason, I hadn't, either, even though I kept thinking about it.

Maybe I should go over to her house now, I thought, glancing up at the copper schooner peeking out over the top of the cliff.

That made me realize another strange thing. Every summer until this one, I'd always headed over to Emma's house first thing in the morning. *Every* morning, just about. But today it hadn't even occurred to me. Was it possible that Emma wasn't the only one who was changing?

The thought made me feel lonely and kind of

itchy inside, as if I wasn't even sure what was what anymore. I stared out at the gently undulating water of the cove—at least that was always the same. Or was it? My science teacher had told us that the Earth's oceans were always circulating water around the globe, which meant a drop of water from Long Island Sound could end up in, I don't know, the waters near the South Pole.

I squinted at the calm water, focusing hard, trying to imagine that. So when a gray fin suddenly broke the surface just a dozen yards away, I was startled enough to let out a gasp.

My heart raced, sure that it was a shark. We didn't see many of those in the cove, but occasionally a small one would wander in.

Then a familiar scarred face emerged, and my face relaxed into a smile.

"Admiral Squeak!" I cried.

The dolphin chirped at me and dove out of sight. I leaped to my feet, wading deeper. A second later, Squeak appeared again a little closer.

"Hey, buddy!" I called, and let out my best dol- phin squeak.

He whistled in reply, and I laughed. I had no idea what he was saying, but it didn't matter. He was back!

I was almost to the drop-off by then. Letting my feet step off into nothingness, I swam out to meet the dolphin. My mother would freak out if she knew what I was doing—we weren't supposed to swim alone.

But I wasn't nervous at all. I was as comfort- able in the water as I was on dry land. Besides, Squeak wouldn't let anything happen to me. Weren't there all kinds of stories about dolphins rescuing struggling swimmers?

I forgot all of that as Squeak whistled at me again. He dove back underwater and I dove under, too, opening my eyes and peering forward through the dusky filtered sunlight. Squeak was swimming away, and I followed, propelling myself forward with a couple of strong whip kicks.

When I ran out of air, I popped to the surface, spitting seawater. A second later, Squeak appeared nearby. He swam toward me, bumping me gently with his nose.

I laughed and reached out to pet him, but the sudden movement startled him and he darted off, disappearing underwater.

"Wait, I'm sorry!" I called, pushing my soggy hair out of my face while my legs churned along beneath me to keep me afloat. Since I hadn't really been planning on swimming, I hadn't bothered to tie my hair up, and it floated all around me like seaweed.

Blinking salt out of my eyes, I looked around, hoping I hadn't scared him off. Several long seconds passed, and I was thinking of diving under to look in the deeper water, when . . .

SPLASH!

There he was! Leaping out of the waves a short distance away, arcing joyfully through the air, and slicing gracefully back into the water. I laughed out loud—I couldn't help it. He was so beautiful!

When his head popped into view a few yards away, I let out a whistle. He chirped back, then let out a few clicks before diving down again. I felt the current swirl past my legs as he swam closer.

I held my breath as his head appeared less than an arm's length from where I was treading water. This time I resisted the urge to touch him, instead letting out a soft whistle, putting everything I was feeling into it. He gazed at me, then sidled closer, ducking his snout toward my face.

"Is it okay?" I whispered, carefully raising one hand while still using the other to help keep myself afloat.

His eyes held mine, and I knew that this time he was ready. Moving slowly, I reached over and touched his face, stroking the rubbery skin. The feel of it reminded me a little of the wet suit Jacob used when he dove for lobsters, only thicker and warmer.

"Hi there," I murmured. "I'm glad you came back." I touched the edge of his scar, then glanced at the still water of the cove. "But where's your pod? Are you here all alone?"

He didn't respond; he just floated there, seeming to enjoy being petted.

We stayed like that for a moment. Then Squeak let out a sharp, joyful whistle and nudged my arm with his snout. The sudden movement startled me, and before I'd recovered, he'd taken off again—this time toward the shallows.

I followed, and for the next few minutes, we played a lopsided game of tag. Every time I got close enough to reach for him, he'd take off again, only now I knew it wasn't because he was scared or startled or nervous. Because each time, he let out a whistle that I somehow knew was the dolphin version of a laugh. Or maybe he was saying, "Neener, neener, can't catch me!" like Will used to do whenever Mom and Dad tried to catch him for a bath.

Either way, he was definitely winning our little game, but I didn't mind a bit. I'd never had so much fun!

"Gotcha!" I cried, lunging forward as he darted past.

My hand actually brushed his side, but only because he'd suddenly stopped swimming and raised his head above the water. A split second later, he'd burst into motion again—this time disappearing completely in the direction of the deeper water.

"Squeak?" I called uncertainly.

I stood up—the water only came to my thighs here—and shaded my eyes as I looked around. But the surface was still; there was no sign of Squeak anywhere.

"Hello?"

I jumped, startled by the voice echoing through the cove. It was someone on the trail—a girl I didn't recognize. She was about halfway down, picking her way carefully around the rocks and bits of scree.

By the time she reached the bottom, I was on the beach, doing my best to squeeze most of the water out of my hair. I could already tell it was going to take forever to get all the tangles out after my bath that night.

But that was okay. It had been worth it. My gaze wandered back out toward the water, wishing this stranger hadn't scared Squeak off just when we were having so much fun.

"Hi!" Speaking of the stranger, she was marching right up to me with a big smile on her face. "I'm Zoe. I just moved in up there."

She waved a slim hand in the direction of the cliff. I blinked at her, finally realizing who she had to be.

"Oh," I said. "You mean Brooke's house."

"I guess so." Zoe shrugged and pushed her glasses up her nose, still smiling. She had a dimple in one cheek, which combined with her bronzy-tan skin and dark eyes to make her look vaguely exotic. "Hey, I love your hair! I've always wanted to grow mine long like that, but I always lose patience and chop it all off before it gets past my chin."

She let out a hearty laugh, tugging on her wavy dark bobbed hair. I smiled weakly, not really in the mood for girl talk, especially with a total stranger. And even more especially with a total stranger who'd just moved into Brooke's old house, which meant she was just another spoiled rich girl who'd probably end up in Morgan's little clique soon enough. Besides all that, I couldn't help feeling annoyed with her for scaring off Admiral Squeak. Would he come back?

I touched my wet hair. "Thanks. Um, but I should probably go comb it out before it dries," I said.

Zoe hardly seemed to hear me. She pushed her glasses up again and peered out toward the water.

"Was there someone else out there with you?" she asked. "I could've sworn I saw two people out there when I started down. By the way, that trail needs a handrail! I thought I was going to die!"

She laughed loudly again, but I had already grabbed my shorts and was heading for the trail. "Nope, it was just me," I said. "Sorry, I really do have to go. It'll be lunchtime soon and my dad will need my help at his restaurant."

"Your dad has his own restaurant?" Zoe looked impressed. "Cool! I wish my dad did something like that. He's a pilot, so he's away, like, all the time. Total bummer, right?"

"Yeah." I kept moving toward the base of the trail. "Nice to meet you. I'm sure I'll see you around sometime."

With that, I bolted up the trail, not looking back.

5

The next day, I didn't make it to the cove at all. Will and I both had dentist's appointments, and as usual, it took twice as long as it should have since Will screamed every time Dr. Abbott tried to go near his mouth. After we finally got out of there, Mom dragged us to the mall, saying that if she had to take a personal day she might as well get all her errands done. I couldn't stop thinking about Squeak as I trailed after her from one boring store to another, trying to stop Will from breaking anything.

By the time we got back to town, it was almost dinner rush, so we'd all gone straight to the restaurant. For once, just about every table was full, which meant Mom and Jacob both had to step in to help the evening waitress while I helped Dad in the kitchen. Will even helped a little by shucking corn for the chowder.

So on Thursday morning, I barely took time to gulp down some juice and half a banana before bolting for the door. "Hey, where are you going?" Will asked, looking up from the comic book Jacob had given him to read over breakfast to keep him quiet. "Can I come?"

I stuck my feet into my flip-flops, which were on the mat beside the back door. "Why do you want to come?" I said. "You don't even know where I'm going."

"I want to come! I want to come!" Will chanted, pounding his fists on the table.

Jacob looked up from his books. "Easy, dude," he said, reaching across the table to grab Will's juice glass just before it tipped over.

Will ignored him, jumping to his feet and

running over to grab my arm. "Let meeeeee come!" he wailed, his voice rising in pitch with each word.

I shook him off a little harder than necessary. "No!" I snapped. "Not if you're going to act like a baby."

"I'm not a baby." Will stuck out his lower lip, wounded. "I'm eight now. Almost a man."

Jacob chuckled, but I just rolled my eyes. "A caveman, maybe," I muttered.

"Are you going for a swim?" Jacob asked me, taking in the swimsuit peeking out from under my clothes. "Maybe Will could come."

"Um, actually I'm just going over to Emma's," I lied, tugging the collar of my T-shirt a little higher over the straps of my swimsuit. "We might swim later, but first we're going to spend a few hours looking at fashion magazines and painting our toenails and stuff."

Jacob raised an eyebrow, looking unconvinced. But my story had worked. Will was making an "ick" face.

"I hate fashion magazines," he declared, flopping back into his seat at the kitchen table. "They're boring."

"Okay. See you." I darted out the door before either of them could say anything else.

I walked across the yard in the direction of Emma's house just in case my brothers were watching out the window. But as soon as I rounded the clump of chokeberry by our mailbox, I veered off toward the cove trail.

Little Twin was deserted except for a crow pecking at a clump of seaweed; as I walked across the beach, the bird flew off with a lazy caw. I peered out at the water as I shrugged off my shorts and T-shirt.

"Come out, come out, wherever you are Admiral Squeak," I singsonged softly. Then I let out a couple of my best dolphin whistles and chirps.

There was no response. The water stayed glassy-calm, revealing no hint of the dolphin's dorsal fin or his scarred, smiling face.

I splashed out through the shallows, then tried my dolphin calls again. Still no response.

Maybe he's sleeping farther out in the cove and didn't hear me, I thought.

Did dolphins sleep? I'd never really thought about it before. But they had to, right?

I whistled again when I reached the drop-off, but there was still no sign of Squeak. Slipping into the deeper water, I dog-paddled out, chirping or whistling every few minutes. But finally I had to give up and accept that Admiral Squeak wasn't around.

As I emerged at the top of the trail a little while later, Emma was just wandering along the road. "Hey!" she greeted me cheerfully, pushing back a strand of long hair that had escaped from her ponytail. "I was just on my way to your house. Want to come over?"

"Sure," I said immediately, relieved that she was acting normal for a change. Maybe this meant that Morgan and her gang had gotten bored with their Cinder Emma project. Maybe they'd finally realized that Emma wasn't like them and never would be, no matter how hard they tried to make her over. Maybe now I could have my best friend back, and things could return to the way they'd always been.

I followed her back along the road, and we pushed through the whitewashed wooden gate separating the sandy, dusty, piney scrublands from the Stewart-Bells' manicured green yard. Emma's mom was at her easel in one of her favorite spots, the shade of the old crab-apple tree along one side of the house, where she had a fantastic view of the harbor where it met the Sound. She heard us coming and looked around.

"Annie!" she exclaimed. "Where have you been, my love? I need your opinion on this shade of blue."

She waved her paintbrush at the canvas she was working on. I stepped forward, studying the painting. Like most of her work, it showed the coastline beyond the Point. Ellery Bell was famous, and she'd made our little corner of Connecticut famous, too. Her gorgeous, moody seascapes hung in galleries and museums all over the world, and everyone in town had read the *New York Times* article that called her the Andrew Wyeth of Connecticut.

I leaned forward as I noticed a detail off to one side of the painting. "Wait, are those—are those dolphins?" I asked, squinting at a couple of tiny blobs of paint.

"Dolphins?" Emma's mom glanced at the picture. "I don't know, I suppose they could be. Really, I just thought the scene needed a little motion, a little life, you know? A hint of the world beneath the waters."

"Come on." Emma grabbed my hand and tugged me toward the house. "We have to go, Mom."

A blast of cold air hit me when we stepped into the house. The Cottage was old, but the Stewart-Bells had outfitted it with all the modern conveniences, from AC to a gourmet kitchen that had made my dad's eyes bug out the few times he'd been inside. My gaze wandered toward the front doors, which opened onto the porch. Maybe Emma and I could plan our beach sleepover today. That might even take my mind off Admiral Squeak for a while.

"Let's go upstairs." Emma opened the giant stainless-steel refrigerator and grabbed a couple of sodas. "I want to show you something."

I followed her up the curving staircase and down the upstairs hallway, which was wider than the entire main room in my house. When she pushed open the door to her bedroom, I blinked in surprise.

"What'd you do to your room?" I exclaimed.

Emma looked pleased as she glanced around. "You like it? I figured it was time for a change."

I wasn't sure what to say. I'd always loved Emma's room. Even though it was four times the size of mine, it had still managed to feel cozy, thanks to her fringed canopy bed, shelves full of books and stuffed animals, posters of animals and flowers on the walls, and colorful mishmash of throw rugs we'd layered over the boring beige carpet.

Now it looked totally different. The posters and most of the stuffed animals were gone, with only a single pale brown teddy bear perched atop the new white bedspread. The canopy bed's wispy curtains had disappeared, too, revealing the stark modern frame. A couple of new posters had replaced the old ones, one of them featuring a moonlit view of the Eiffel Tower and another a popular boy band.

I stood in the doorway feeling a little dizzy at all the changes. Emma didn't seem to notice my reaction. She set the sodas on her desk, then reached down to grab something on the far side of her bed.

"Check it out," she said.

Tearing my gaze away from the Eiffel Tower, I saw that she was holding a shiny reddish-brown guitar. She strummed a loud chord.

"What's that?" I asked.

"My new guitar. Isn't it cool?" She adjusted her fingers on the frets and strummed a different chord, softer this time. "Connor's older brother helped me pick it out. He's in, like, a real band."

"Since when do you play the guitar?" I demanded. "You play the oboe."

She shrugged, fiddling with the strings. "I was getting kind of bored with that. I thought it was time for a change."

She seemed to be saying that sort of thing a lot lately. And I didn't like it. Emma had been playing the oboe forever. That was her thing at school, just like swim team was my thing.

Bending over the instrument, she picked out a series of notes. It sounded kind of off-key to me, but she smiled. "Anyway, guitar is much cooler than oboe."

"Says who?" I probably sounded a little aggressive, but I didn't care.

Anyway, Emma didn't seem to notice. "Everyone," she said with another shrug. "Morgan. Connor's brother. You know."

I wasn't sure what to say to that. Once again I found myself wondering: Why does she care what Morgan thinks?

"Well, I don't want to sit around listening to you practice," I said. "Besides, it's freezing in here. Let's go play tennis or something."

Spinning around, I headed for the stairs. Halfway down, I heard Emma clattering after me.

"Wait up," she said. "Are you sure you want to play tennis? It's so hot today."

"I'm sure." Somehow, knowing that she didn't want to play made me even more determined.

Soon we were out on the clay court in the side yard between the Cottage and the tall evergreen hedge that marked the property line with Morgan's house, lobbing a ball back and forth. It was pretty steamy out there, but I didn't mind. Summer was supposed to be hot.

I was winding up for a serve when I heard a sharp, eager bark somewhere behind me. Glancing over my shoulder at the arched wooden gateway in the hedge, I saw Zoe, the girl I'd met in the cove. Dragging her along at the end of its leash was the cutest little dog I'd ever seen. He was small and furry and brown, with a pointy nose and ears that went in two different directions.

"Hi!" Zoe called breathlessly, trying to keep up as her dog yanked her toward us. "Bongo wanted to go visiting, and there was nobody home next door, and I heard voices over here—I hope it's okay that we came through this way. Go say hi, Bongo boy." She bent and unclipped the leash from the dog's collar. As soon as he was free, he barked again and leaped toward me.

Emma watched as Bongo jumped up on my legs. "What kind of dog is he? I've never seen a breed like that."

Zoe laughed and poked her glasses up her nose. "Oh, he's not any breed in particular. Actually my mom says he's probably got a little bit of everything in him. Including a little pig—he eats like one, anyway."

"He's adorable." I dropped my racket and kneeled down to rub the dog's floppy ears. "I like his name, too."

"Thanks." Zoe's smile was wide and friendly. "Speaking of names, you never told me yours the other day. But don't worry, I figured it out. You're Annie Reed, right? You live in that cute little house in the woods?"

"Right. Sorry I ran off like that. Um, I was kind of distracted." I found myself mesmerized by her dimple, which grew deeper when she smiled. "Uh, this is Emma Stewart-Bell."

"Yeah, we've met." Emma sounded a little grumpy. She also wasn't coming over to meet Bongo, which was strange, since she loved animals just as much as I did.

"Right, Emma's folks had us over the other day," Zoe said. "I still think it's totally cool that I'm going to be living almost right next door to a famous artist!"

I glanced up at Emma in surprise. She hadn't mentioned meeting Zoe. That was weird, especially since she'd been so curious about her at Will's birthday party on Friday.

"So that place where you were swimming the other day," Zoe said. "What's the deal? Is it, you know, private property or what?"

I giggled as Bongo's little pink tongue darted out, sloshing across my nose and cheek. "Little Twin?" I said. "No, it's public, but nobody goes there except from right here on the Point, so it practically feels like our own private beach."

"It's amazing," Zoe said. "I love the tide pool there—I spent like an hour staring into it after you left. See, I want to be a marine biologist someday, maybe. At least I'm thinking about it."

"There's always tons of fish and animals in the

cove," I replied, playing with Bongo's ears. "We even saw a dolphin there last week."

"Annie!" Emma hissed, her eyes widening.

Oops. Zoe was so friendly and nice that I'd forgotten Admiral Squeak was supposed to be a secret. But so what? It wasn't as if I'd told her his name, so there was no way she could spill the beans to Morgan even if they did end up being friends.

"A dolphin?" Zoe's eyes widened behind her glasses. "So cool! I love dolphins. I did a whole report on them a couple of years ago. Did you know they do something called a signature whistle? At least I think that's what it's called. It's like a special little song, and they think it's how dolphins recognize one another. Or something." She scratched her ear. "The report was a few years ago, so I can't remember all the details anymore."

"Really?" I thought about the sounds Squeak had made, especially the funny little whistle-chirp he'd done several times while we were playing in the water on Tuesday. I just hoped I'd get another chance to hear it. Which reminded me . . . "Do you know if dolphins, um, sleep?" I asked.

Emma stared at me. "Of course they do," she said. "Every animal has to sleep, right?"

"I'm not sure." Zoe swung Bongo's leash around her hand. "I don't remember everything. Maybe I could dig out my old report and see if it says." She laughed. "You know—once we actually get all the boxes unpacked."

"Sure." I wasn't going to hold my breath on that. Zoe seemed pretty cool now. But as soon as she settled in, I was sure she'd glom on to Morgan and the other rich girls and forget all about me.

Still, she'd made me realize there was a lot I didn't know about dolphins. Maybe I could look up some information on the computer later. If I could get near it, anyway. Jacob tended to hog it all the time lately to search for information on college applications and scholarships and stuff.

Or maybe I'll check the library, I thought, standing up as Bongo bounded over to say hello to Emma.

The town library was a quaint little place located in the decommissioned lighthouse at the mouth of the harbor. Most people probably saw it as nothing more than a cute photo op, but it actually had a pretty good collection, including lots of books on local history, nautical stuff, and marine biology. At least that was what Jacob had told me once after doing some research there for a school project. Maybe Emma and I could bike down there today.

I shot a sidelong look at Zoe, wondering if I should invite her to join us. Before I could decide, I heard someone calling her name. A moment later, a pretty young woman with thick, wavy dark hair burst in through the gate in the hedge.

"There you are!" she called, hurrying toward us. "I thought you'd fallen into the sea."

Zoe laughed. "Sorry, Marta." She waved a hand at Emma and me, introducing us. "This is Marta, my nanny," she told us after that. "Well, she's mostly my little sister's nanny now. But she treats me like I'm four years old, too."

Both she and Marta laughed at that, and then Marta muttered something under her breath in what sounded like another language. Whatever she'd said made Zoe laugh again.

"Marta's from Spain, in case you were wondering," she said.

That brought me back to reality. Zoe's dad was an airline pilot, and she had a nanny from Spain, and she was rich enough to live in Brooke's old house with its pool and fitness room and air-conditioned garage. Maybe it was better if I didn't invite her to the library—or anywhere else—after all. As nice as Zoe seemed, I had to remember that she came from a different world from mine. Maybe too different.

After she and Marta and Bongo left, Emma bounced the tennis ball with her racket. "So I meant to tell you about her," she said, glancing toward the hedge to make sure the other girl was really gone. "Or should I say warn you about her?"

"Warn me? Why?" I was distracted, thinking about what Zoe had said about dolphins' signature whistles.

"Morgan says she's a wack job." Emma lobbed the ball across the net, where it bounced off to the side and rolled up against the fence. "She heard she got kicked out of her school in New York for, like, selling drugs or something? I don't know, maybe it wasn't that, but she's trouble, anyway. And her mom is some kind of super-rich heiress who likes to flit all around the world and dump her kids on the nanny."

"Really?" I wasn't sure I trusted anything Morgan said. But it didn't matter. I was already planning to keep my distance from Zoe, especially since Emma seemed to be planning to do the same thing. Sure, Zoe seemed okay so far—nicer than Brooke, anyway, that was for sure. But the last thing I needed right now was another rich girl coming between me and my best friend.

6

Crystal the waitress was sick all weekend—or so she claimed when she called off, anyway—so the whole family was pretty busy for a while. I wasn't allowed to actually work as a waitress since I was too young, but I could wash dishes and watch Will and fetch stuff from the pantry as well as anyone else.

On Sunday afternoon, I was stacking clean plates on a shelf over the flat-top grill when my dad stepped over and patted me on the back. "Thanks for pitching in this weekend, Snappy," he said. "I know you'd probably rather be hanging out at the cove with Emma."

I smiled weakly. I hadn't seen Emma since our tennis game on Thursday. That was weird, but I was trying not to think about it. After all, I'd been busy here, so even if she'd stopped by my house a dozen times, she might have missed me.

"It's okay," I told Dad. I finished with the plates and then turned to face him. "Actually, I have been going down to the cove as often as I can. But I haven't seen Squeak again at all."

I'd told my family about seeing the friendly dolphin last week, though I'd left out the part about playing with him in the deep water. I definitely didn't need Mom to freak out and ban me from the cove for swimming alone.

Anyway, I wasn't technically alone, I'd reminded myself. *I was with Squeak.*

Dad scratched his chin, looking thoughtful. "I see," he said. "Well, I suppose we shouldn't be too surprised, hmm? He probably headed back to warmer waters as soon as he could. Especially if he missed his pod."

My heart sank. "Do you really think so?"

"I don't know." He squeezed my shoulder, his eyes gentle. "But you know the sea is always changing, and all its creatures, too. Dolphins don't come here very often, especially on their own. Maybe we need to focus on how special it was that Squeak was here at all, rather than being sad that he seems to have moved on."

Just then, Jacob crashed in asking if the next order was ready yet, and Dad hurried off. But I couldn't stop thinking about what he'd said for the rest of the day—or that evening, either, as I sat on the beach staring out at the empty waters of the cove.

On Tuesday morning, Dad told us kids we all had the day off. Crystal was back, and weekdays weren't that busy at the restaurant anyway.

So I pulled my hair back in a ponytail and grabbed my sneakers from the bin in the coat closet, sitting down by the back door to put them on.

Jacob looked up from his books, which were spread all over the table. "What, no flip-flops today?" he joked.

"I want to go to the library, and I hate riding my bike in flip-flops," I said, carefully double-knotting my laces so they wouldn't catch in the spokes.

"The library?" Will had finished his breakfast and was playing with his Legos in the corner. I hadn't even realized he was listening, but now he rushed over to me. "I want to come, too!"

I frowned, shooting my older brother a look. "I thought you and Jacob were going body surfing in the cove today."

"Library! Library!" Will chanted. "I can ride my bike with you!"

"No way," I said. "Last time you rode your bike to town, you almost steered right into the harbor!"

Jacob chuckled. "Here's an idea, bud," he said to Will. "How about we go with Annie, but we walk to the library instead of ride?"

Will brightened immediately. "Yeah!" he cheered.

"What?" I cried at the same time.

Jacob shrugged and smiled, pushing back from the table. "I could use a break from studying," he told me. "Besides, I was thinking about hitting up the library soon anyway—I heard they got in the new study guides I was looking for."

I gritted my teeth, wanting to argue but knowing there was no point. Will was already jumping into his flip-flops, and Jacob had that look on his face that said his mind was made up. If I wanted to go to the library that morning, I was going to have company.

It took almost half an hour to hike down to the library, even though we took a shortcut trail through the pines to avoid the big loop the road had to take around the swampy area just behind the Point. By the time we hit the harbor, my pony-tail was limp and my feet were sweating buckets inside my sneakers—plus I was pretty sure I was growing a blister on my left big toe.

It took another fifteen minutes to walk around to the opposite side of the harbor. Tons of tourists were strolling around over there as usual, and it looked like all the outside tables at the Dockview were already full, even though it was the middle of the morning. As we passed the place, I glanced across the water toward Dad's restaurant, but it was mostly invisible behind the maze of masts and sails in the marina.

We kept going, passing antique shops, souvenir stands, and more. Will tried to convince Jacob to buy him something at every food place we passed, from the popcorn stall to the ice cream parlor to the fish-and-chips place, but Jacob wheedled him past all of them somehow.

The lighthouse library was out at the far end of the harbor, where the water spilled into the Sound.

When we finally got there, an older couple was snapping selfies in front of the picturesque building. The woman smiled at us, and her husband lowered his phone and hurried forward.

"Hello there, kids," he said in that friendly, jovial, overly loud tone a lot of tourists used, like they wanted to make sure everyone knew they were having fun. "You from around here?"

"Uh-huh." Jacob smiled back. "Something we can help you with?"

The woman nodded and came forward to join her husband, squinting at us over the rims of her oversized sunglasses. "We heard there's a wonderful seafood restaurant in this town," she said.

I opened my mouth to tell them about Dad's restaurant. But the man was already talking again.

"Yes, we saw it on a website—it's called the Dockside, I believe?" he said.

"The Dockview." Jacob's smile didn't waver. Lifting his left hand, he pointed back in the direction we'd just come from. "It's that way, just before you hit the marina—you can't miss it."

"Thanks, son," the man said, but his wife just raised her eyebrows and turned away quickly as she caught a glimpse of Jacob's missing fingers. I winced, but as usual, Jacob didn't seem to notice.

"Enjoy your day," he said to the couple.

Will had been staring at the tourists like they were some kind of museum exhibit, but now he was clearly getting bored. He dodged around them, bumping into the man as he passed, and yanked open the library door. I shot the husband a small smile, ignoring his wife. Then I followed my brothers inside.

It felt cool and dim and dry in there after the bright, sticky summer heat outside. Jacob nodded to the librarian, a prune-faced old man with a goatee who was perched on a stool behind the counter reading a book.

Meanwhile, Will let out a gasp and pointed at one of the large framed photographs hanging behind the counter. "Look!" he exclaimed. "It's Admiral Squeak!"

Years ago, Morgan's father had put up most of the money to convert the lighthouse into a library. To thank him and the other rich people who'd chipped in, they'd put up a whole row of those framed photos. But Admiral Zeke's was bigger than the others and had a place of honor right in the middle, his scarred, handsome face gazing out over the lobby.

"Hush," Jacob told Will, clamping a hand on his shoulder as the librarian shot us all a withering look. "Come on, let's go check out the kids' books."

Will shrugged off his grip, prancing around in circles and flapping his arms at his shoulders like fins. "Look at me, I'm Admiral Squeak!" he cried. "Squeak! Squeak! Squeak!"

"Will, quit it!" I hissed, trying to grab him as he "swam" past.

But he knocked my arm away, his fingers tangling in my hair and almost yanking my ponytail loose.

"Stay away!" he cried. "Squeaky dolphins have to be free!"

I winced as the librarian set down his book and frowned. At that moment, the door swung open, letting in a blast of warm summer air along with the tourist couple we'd talked to outside.

"Hello there," the husband said. "Is this—"

"Oh my!" his wife exclaimed as Will crashed into her.

"Enough!" The librarian strode out from behind his desk. He scowled at Jacob, then at me, pointing one knobby finger toward the door. "Out."

"Sorry." Jacob grabbed Will by the elbow. "We're going."

"Hey!" Will protested.

But this time, Jacob didn't let him squirm away. I slunk after them as they hurried out, trying not to listen as the librarian started apologizing to the tourists.

"Let go!" Will yelled as we emerged. He thrashed around until Jacob finally released him.

"Thanks a lot, Will," I said, feeling grumpy. "We'll be lucky if any of us are ever allowed back in there again."

"It's not my fault."

"So whose fault is it?" I snapped back.

"Enough!" Jacob interrupted. "Look, guys, what's done is done. Let's not ruin the rest of the day by fighting, okay?"

That sounded like something Dad would say. I frowned at my brother, not sure I was in the mood to do anything but fight just then. Realizing my ponytail was a lost cause, I pulled the elastic out and tried to smooth my hair down as best I could.

"How about some ice cream?" Jacob turned to Will with a smile. "My treat."

"Yay!" Will pumped his fist, instantly happy again. "Can I have five scoops?"

Jacob chuckled. "How about two?"

"Okay!" Will scampered off down the sidewalk.

Jacob and I followed. "You shouldn't bribe him

into acting like a normal person," I grumbled. "Or if you do, you should at least do it before he gets us kicked out of places."

He sighed. "Whatever, Annie." He let out a whistle. "Will! Wait for us."

We'd just about reached the ice cream place when the door swung open, the little bell jangling merrily. My face went tight as Morgan stepped out—immediately followed by Emma. Both of them were holding cones that were already dripping down over their hands in the heat.

If Jacob thought it was weird to see them together, he didn't show it. "Hi, girls," he greeted them cheerfully. "Good day for ice cream, huh?"

"Sure." Morgan licked her cone, surveying me through her sunglasses. "Interesting hairstyle, Annie."

My cheeks burned as I quickly lifted my hands to my messy hair, not that there was much I could do until I got a comb and a mirror. Morgan smirked and turned away.

"You'll have to excuse us," she told Jacob with a toss of her own flawlessly styled short hair. "We've got to get down to the marina."

"Oh yeah? What are you up to?" I could tell Jacob was just being polite—most of his attention was on Will, who was trying to sidle past Morgan into the ice cream parlor.

But I was more focused on Emma. Why in the world was she hanging out with Morgan—again?

"We're going Jet Skiing," Emma spoke up.

"What?" I'd almost forgotten about the last time she and Morgan had talked about Jet Skiing. Since Emma hadn't said anything about it, I'd sort of assumed she'd chickened out and decided not to do it after all.

"Yeah," Morgan said, twisting her hand around to catch a drip on the far side of her cone. "We had such a blast the other day that we begged Connor and the guys to let us go again."

Emma giggled. "Don't you mean *they* begged us?"

My eyes narrowed. Who was this girl standing in front of me, and what had she done with my best friend? Because the real Emma wouldn't be giggling with Morgan Pierce over some stupid boys. Especially creepy Connor Sullivan and his friends.

"Anyway, we should go," Morgan said. "And you should probably go to the hairdresser, Annie. Didn't anyone tell you that long hair is totally third grade?"

Jacob looked confused, as if he wasn't quite sure whether she was joking. Meanwhile, Emma bit her lip, looking a little unhappy.

"Stop, Morgan," she said, nudging her with her elbow. "But yeah, we should go. See you guys, okay?"

"Bye," Jacob said.

But I couldn't say a word. I just stared after Emma until she and Morgan disappeared into the throngs of people around the marina.

7

By Saturday, I'd almost given up hope of Squeak coming back. Still, I couldn't resist heading down to the cove after lunch—just in case. I'd biked down to the library that morning and picked up a book about dolphins. Now, having slipped away while Will was distracted by the TV, I hurried toward the trail, looking forward to sitting in the shallows and reading.

About halfway down, I heard footsteps on the trail behind me. For a split second, I was sure it had to be Emma. I hadn't seen her since the other day at the ice cream place, but maybe she'd finally come to her senses. Maybe she'd seen me head down here and followed me, wanting to apologize. Maybe things could finally go back to the way they should be.

I turned with a smile, my mouth already opening to greet her. But I snapped it shut when I saw my little brother skidding down the hilly trail toward me.

"Hi," Will said brightly. "Are you going to the beach? I'm coming, too—Jacob said I could."

I frowned, wondering if he was telling the truth. Either way, it seemed like too much trouble to climb back up to the house. If Jacob missed Will, he'd probably figure out where to look.

"Whatever," I said. "Just don't expect me to entertain you, okay? And you can't go in past your toes since you didn't bring your life jacket."

"Okay." Will pushed past me, slipping and sliding the rest of the way down the steep trail.

I stepped on the beach just in time to see him heading for the water. "Stop!" I commanded. "You can't go in, remember? Not unless you go back to the house and get your life jacket."

Will frowned but stepped back. "Okay," he said. "I'm going to look for interesting stones."

"Fine." I kicked off my flip-flops and stepped into the shallows. The water felt cool and welcome on my feet and ankles. Realizing I still had my shorts on, I was about to turn back to shore to shuck them when a flash of movement caught my eye farther out.

Shading my eyes with my hand, I peered out there. For a second, I didn't see anything. Then I gasped as a familiar sleek gray shape burst out of the water, leaping and twisting in the air before splashing down again.

"Squeak!" I exclaimed, my heart thumping. I hadn't had a good look at the dolphin's face, but I was sure it was him.

"Where?" Will rushed forward, dropping the rock he'd just picked up.

"Stop!" I told him, quickly wading back to dry

land. Shedding my shorts as quickly as I could, I handed him my book. "Stay here," I ordered. "I'll be right back."

"But—" Will began.

"Just do it!"

I hurried back into the water. Squeak came to meet me as I reached the drop-off and started to swim. I smiled as his scarred face popped out of the water.

"Hey, buddy," I said. "I was afraid you were never coming back!"

The dolphin whistled, then dove under, brushing against me as he passed.

I smiled, reaching toward him, but he was already gone. He surfaced again several yards away, leaping out of the water.

"Wait up!" I cried, diving under myself and skimming along just under the surface. I had my eyes open, but I couldn't see Squeak anywhere.

Suddenly I felt something bump me from

beneath. I rolled to the side as Squeak burst out of the water, twisting in the air and landing nearby.

"Hey!" I cried, laughing and spitting out water from the splash. "Don't land on me!"

I waited for him to surface, but there was no sign of him. When I glanced around, I saw him several yards behind me, completely ignoring me as he floated there facing toward shore.

"Squeak?" I called, striking out toward him. When I reached him, I tweaked his fin. "Tag, you're it!" I said with a laugh.

He jerked away, letting out a sharp whistle. Then he sped toward shore, his dorsal fin cutting the water.

Where was he going, and why was he acting so strangely all of a sudden? As I looked past him, I finally noticed Will. He wasn't on the beach where I'd left him—he was wading far out through the shallows, the water up over his waist.

"Will!" I shouted. "Stop right there!"

My little brother hesitated for a moment, squinting out toward me. "Here, Admiral Squeak!" his voice drifted toward me on the breeze.

Then he took another step and wobbled. "No!" I yelled, my voice cracking with panic as I realized he'd just reached the drop-off. "Will, stop! I mean it!"

It was too late. With a cry, he toppled into the deeper water. His arms flailed, and he shrieked with fear. Soon his bright reddish-blond head disappeared beneath the waves.

I kicked off and swam as fast as I could. Luckily I hadn't been too far out. I reached him just as he was about to go under again, flinging one arm around his chest and tipping him back the way I'd learned from Dad.

"Annie!" he burbled, water spurting out of his mouth and nose.

"Don't talk," I said breathlessly. "Just stay still."

It was only a few feet back to the drop-off. Soon I was able to put my feet down, and half carry and half lead Will back to the beach.

He collapsed onto the rocky sand, still coughing and sputtering. I leaned over, resting my hands on my knees as I waited for my breath to come back and my heart to slow down.

Finally I was able to speak. "I told you not to go in!" I yelled, my insides a churning mess of relief combined with anger and maybe a touch of guilt. "You could have drowned!"

He tilted his head up at me, looking a little scared but mostly sullen. "I wanted to play with Admiral Squeak, too," he said. "I'm the one who named him, remember?"

That reminded me to glance out at the water. But Squeak was nowhere in sight. Had Will's thrashing and screaming scared him out of the cove?

I wanted to swim back out to look for him, but I didn't dare. Not with Will here, anyway.

"Come on." I grabbed his hand, dragging him to his feet. "I'm taking you home."

Half an hour later, I was making my way down the cove trail again. Needless to say, Jacob hadn't been happy about what had happened. He'd tried to insist that both Will and I stay in the house for the rest of the afternoon.

But I wanted to see if Squeak was still in the cove. Besides, I'd been in such a hurry to get Will home that I'd forgotten my shorts and library book down on the beach. Even Jacob agreed that I should retrieve the book, so he distracted Will with a video game long enough for me to slip out.

Halfway down, I heard the sound of whistling. It was Emma! She was down on the beach, bent over something in the rocky area near the tidal pool.

"Hey!" I called, hurrying the rest of the way down. "Emma!"

She looked up, and I realized she'd been peering at her smartphone, a gift from her parents on her last birthday. The shade from the cliffs hid her expression, but when she stepped into the sunlight, I could see that she was frowning slightly. I also noticed a battered metal bucket sitting on the sand nearby—the same one we always used to collect shells and stuff.

"Annie," she said. "I didn't know you were coming down."

I laughed. "Since when do we have to make an appointment to come here?" My mood had lifted just seeing her here in our favorite spot. Until that moment, I hadn't even realized how much I'd missed her over the past few days. "Where have you been hiding lately, anyway?"

She shrugged, fiddling with her phone. "Oh, you know. Here and there."

I stepped forward and glanced into the bucket. It was half full of rocks and sand. "What are you doing?"

She glanced down at the bucket, then tugged on a strand of her long hair, something she only did when she was nervous. But what did she have to be nervous about, just standing there talking to me?

"Um, actually it's lucky I ran into you," she said in a fast, breathy sort of voice. "See, Morgan and I were planning a beach sleepover tonight, and I wanted to see if you wanted to come, too."

My whole body went numb, and for a second it felt like I forgot how to breathe. A beach sleepover . . . with *Morgan*?

"It'll be fun, right?" Emma was smiling at me now, though her eyes still looked worried. "You'll come, won't you?"

I opened my mouth, ready to say yes, of course I'd come. I hadn't missed one of our beach sleepovers in the past five years. Why would I start now?

But I stopped myself before the words came out. This wasn't going to be one of *our* beach sleepovers. Not if Morgan was there.

Besides, a sneaky little thought popped into my mind, *if I hadn't turned up here right now, would Emma have invited me at all? Would she rather it was just her and Morgan?*

The thought was too horrible to bear. "Sorry," I blurted out, willing the tears welling up in my eyes to stay back. "I can't. I'm busy."

Not waiting for a response, I kicked off my flip-flops and raced into the water, flinging myself in to swim as soon as it was deep enough. My arms pulled through the water with powerful strokes, and soon I was halfway to the mouth of the cove.

Only then did I stop for breath. Treading water, I glanced back and saw that Emma had returned to collecting rocks and shells in her bucket. Wasn't she even going to try to follow me?

Guess not, I thought, realizing she'd been wearing shorts and a halter top—no swimsuit in sight.

I forgot about that as I felt something brush against my leg underwater. With a gasp, I pushed back, visions of sharks and jellyfish dancing through my head. But a second later, Squeak's face popped into view, and he let out a cheerful whistle.

I whistled back, my face relaxing into a tiny smile.

"You didn't leave," I said. "And, hey, thanks for warning me about Will earlier."

I lifted a hand, waiting to see how the dolphin would react. He stayed where he was, letting out a soft chirp, so I reached over and stroked him.

He pushed against my hand, floating a little closer. Glancing over my shoulder, I saw that Emma had come to the edge of the water and was looking our way.

That made me feel daring somehow, and I ran my hand over Squeak's head and along his back toward his dorsal fin. He moved away before I touched it, letting out another chirp.

"Sorry," I said. "Don't you want me to touch your fin?"

At the sound of my voice, he swam closer again.

This time when I reached for his fin, he didn't swim away. I touched it, then gripped it a little more tightly. I'd seen those shows where people held on to trained dolphins and got pulled around like Emma had talked about the first time we'd seen Squeak. But I wasn't sure how a wild dolphin might react if I tried it.

Squeak didn't seem to know how to react, either. He just floated there for a moment, rolling his eyes back toward me.

"Go ahead, buddy," I urged. "Let's swim!"

I kicked my legs, pushing him sideways. That got him started, and he dove under the water so quickly I hardly had time to take a breath. I held on for a few seconds, then lost my grip, clawing my way back to the surface and emerging laughing and sputtering.

The dolphin popped up nearby seeming to grin at me. "That was quite a ride, Squeak," I exclaimed, feeling breathless—partly just from being underwater, but mostly because those few seconds had felt like flying. Amazing! "Can we try it again? Maybe a little slower this time, huh?"

For half an hour or so after that, we played at dolphin rides. The next few times went much like the first, but eventually we both got the hang of it. By the end, Squeak was dragging me halfway across the cove before I lost my grip. I sort of wished the other kids from the swim team could see me now. They'd known I was fast before, but with Squeak I was unbeatable!

I was having so much fun that I forgot to keep sneaking peeks toward the beach, so I wasn't quite sure when Emma left. But by the time I retreated to the shallows to catch my breath, she was nowhere to be seen. I tried not to let myself feel sad about that.

"Who needs her?" I muttered, watching as Squeak swam around just beyond the drop-off. "At least I still have one friend, even if he talks in squeaks and whistles and lives in the water."

8

I woke up early on Monday after a night of restless dreams where I was a mermaid and lived underwater with Squeak and coached a swim team made up of crabs and jellyfish. Or something like that, anyway—as usual the details soon drifted away, but the mood of the dream stuck with me for a while.

After a quick breakfast consisting of a glass of milk and a handful of grapes, I stepped into my flip-flops and headed for the door. I hadn't been to the cove the day before, since I'd spent the entire day helping at the restaurant and trying not to think about Emma's sleepover.

It didn't really work, though. Everything I was trying so hard not to think about kept crowding into my mind, especially since there were hardly any customers to distract me.

There was only one thing I thought might make me feel better—seeing Squeak. There was no chance I'd run into Emma down at the cove this early. Or anyone else, either.

As I pushed open the door, I heard the clatter of footsteps on the steps behind me. It was Dad.

"Snappy!" he said. "Glad I caught you. Got any big plans today?"

I let the door swing shut again, wondering what Monday errand he wanted my help with. "Not really," I said. "I was just going down to the cove."

"I've got a better idea." He headed over and started fiddling with the coffee maker. "How about we take the boat out this morning? Maybe we can find that friendly dolphin of yours if he's still around."

"Oh." With a pang of guilt, I realized I'd never told him or Mom about seeing Squeak on Saturday afternoon. Obviously Will hadn't said anything, either, which was a little surprising since he couldn't keep his mouth shut about anything.

Then again, maybe not so surprising. He probably hadn't wanted to get in trouble for going in the water without his life jacket. I still shivered when I remembered how close Will had come to drowning, and wondered if I should tell Dad about the incident now.

But what good would that do? They already knew Will couldn't be trusted in the water, so all it would do was get me and Jacob in trouble for not watching him more closely. And why ruin Dad's mood for no reason—especially if he actually wanted to do something fun on his day off for once instead of more work, work, work?

"Sure, that sounds great," I told him. "I'll get my boat shoes."

An hour later, we were chugging out of our slip in the marina. It was an overcast day, but instead of making it cooler, the low-hanging clouds just seemed to press the humidity closer to earth and make everything feel warm and sticky. My life jacket stuck to my skin, and tendrils of damp hair tickled the back of my neck. I was glad when we reached open water and picked up a little speed—especially since Dad let me drive most of the way to the cove. On the way, we talked about dolphins and the restaurant and other stuff. It was nice.

When we were almost there, Dad took over the controls again. He slowed to a crawl, put-putting toward the opening of the cove.

Suddenly I heard the roar of motors behind us, coming up fast. When I looked back, three large Jet Skis were zipping along over the waves.

They slowed as they came closer. Teenage boys were driving all three of the machines, with girls hanging on behind two of them. I recognized Morgan as one of the girls, her blond hair gleaming in the sun as she clung tightly to Connor Sullivan's waist.

When I glanced at the second girl, I wasn't sure who it was at first. I blinked salt spray out of my eyes, wondering if it could be the new girl, Zoe. Her hair was about the right color and length.

The Jet Skis slowed to an idle, pulling alongside our boat. "Emma!" Dad said with a smile. "Is that you? I thought you didn't like Jet Skis."

I gasped as I realized he was right. The second girl wasn't Zoe—it was Emma! But what had happened to her hair? The last time I'd seen her, it had been nearly as long as mine. And now . . .

Morgan noticed me staring. "What do you think, Annie?" she said with a smug little smile. "I cut Em's hair for her at our sleepover the other night. Doesn't it look way more stylish now?"

She shot a pointed look at my own long braids, but I hardly noticed. I was thinking about that day back in second grade when Emma and I had vowed to grow our hair all the way to our ankles. Okay, so mine had never quite made it below my waist, and Emma usually got frustrated with her split ends and ended up trimming it somewhere around the middle of her back. Still, we'd both been proud of our long hair all these years. I couldn't believe she'd just let Morgan chop it all off without even telling me first!

Emma loosened her grip on Connor's friend, touching the ends of her hair, which barely reached her chin.

"It looks cool, right?" she said.

"Very nice." Dad didn't seem to notice my consternation. "Enjoy your ride, kids. Want to get going again, Annie?" He gestured at the controls.

"Sure." I didn't look at Dad as the whole group sped off. Instead I twisted the starter—a little too vigorously, maybe. The engine sputtered but didn't turn over.

"Easy, Snappy," Dad said, putting his hand over mine to stop me from trying again. "Her engine's a little older and more temperamental than our other boat. You don't want to flood it."

I let go and flopped back as he gently coaxed the engine back to life. I missed our old boat. I missed my best friend and her long hair and not having Morgan hanging around all the time. Basically I missed the way everything used to be before this stupid summer.

It was hard to concentrate on having fun after that, especially since Dad and I never did see Squeak or any other dolphins, though we saw a bunch of fish, and a big ray, and some moon jellies, and even a tiny dogfish shark. Normally that would have been a good day on the water, but somehow today it didn't feel so great. After we returned the boat to the marina, Dad headed over to the restaurant to check on something or other. I should have known he couldn't stay away all day.

I was wandering along toward the road home, kicking at a stone on the sidewalk, when I heard someone call my name up ahead. It was Zoe.

She hurried toward me with Bongo frolicking along beside her. "Hi," I said when they reached me, bending down to pat the friendly little dog.

"What's up, Annie?" Zoe sounded as cheerful as always.

"Just on my way home, actually." I hoped she took the hint. After the morning I'd had, I wasn't really in the mood to socialize.

"Cool, I'll go with you. It's way too hot to walk any farther, right, Bongo?" She bent and ruffled the dog's ears, then glanced up at me over the tops of her glasses, which had slid halfway down her nose. "Hey, didn't you say you saw a dolphin in one of the coves?"

I blinked, startled by the sudden change of topic. "Um, yeah?"

"Did the one you saw look injured? Because everyone's talking about that one."

"Injured?" My heart skipped a beat. Had something happened to Squeak? "What are you talking about?"

"Check it out." She dug a smartphone out of the pocket of her shorts and poked a few buttons on the screen. "Right here."

I peered at the tiny screen. It showed the logo of the local news site. Right below that was a head-line: SCARRED DOLPHIN VISITS LITTLE TWIN COVE.

"What?" I exclaimed, instantly recognizing Squeak in the two photos below the headline. His head was poking out of the water in both of them, clearly showing his scar. "How . . ."

My gaze hit the words under the photos. CREDIT: MORGAN PIERCE.

I stared at Morgan's name, my head spinning. How in the world had she gotten those pictures of Squeak?

Emma.

Suddenly I knew that had to be it. Emma had been holding her smartphone when Squeak had turned up in the cove the other day. She must have snapped some photos while he and I were playing.

That didn't explain how they'd ended up on the news site. But I had a pretty good theory about that, too.

"I didn't even know Morgan's mom was a TV newswoman until now," Zoe commented, scrolling down to the brief article beneath the photos. "I haven't had much chance to talk to Morgan yet. She seems nice, though."

Shows what you know, I wanted to say, though I held my tongue.

"Um, yeah," I said instead.

I stared at the photos, not quite believing this was really happening. I mean, it wasn't hard to believe that Morgan would pull something like this—claiming credit for pictures someone else had taken was right up her alley. It wasn't even that surprising that Emma would let her do it.

The part that was hard to believe? That Emma had broken her promise not to tell Morgan about Squeak.

"I can't believe her," I muttered, anger bubbling up in me.

Zoe glanced at me. "Huh?"

"Nothing." I clenched my fists, glaring up toward the Point. "I have to go."

I took off at a run, quickly leaving behind Zoe's confused shouts and Bongo's excited barking. Halfway up the first hill, I was panting and hot and had to slow to a jog. But my fury kept me going all the way up to the Point.

Emma was lying on a chaise longue in the backyard flipping through a magazine when I stormed in through the gate. "I can't believe you!" I shouted.

She sat up, looking startled. "Annie?"

"How could you do it?" I yelled. "You told Morgan about Squeak after you promised not to!"

"I'm sorry," she said quickly, twisting the magazine between her hands. "It was an accident."

I stared at her. "An accident?!" I exclaimed.

"How can giving away a friend's secret be an accident?!"

"I swear it was!" Looking upset, she reached up as if to give her long hair a tug, then realized it wasn't there anymore and let her hand fall back in her lap. "Morgan wanted to take some pictures of my new haircut, but her camera battery was low. So she used mine, and she was scrolling back through my pictures and saw the ones I took the other day."

"And then you told her all about Squeak." I glared at her.

"What was I supposed to do?" she cried. "You don't see that many dolphins around here, right? Anyway, Morgan emailed the pictures to herself before I could stop her."

"Whatever." I stalked around the yard, still too angry to stand still. "If you hadn't invited her to a sleepover in the first place, it wouldn't have happened."

"Is that what this is about?" She tossed her magazine aside and stood up. "Look, Annie, there's no law that says I can't have other friends."

That stopped me short. "I never said that," I told her through gritted teeth. "But why'd you have to pick *Morgan*?"

"Why not?" she shot back, her cheeks going pink. "She's a lot nicer than you think."

"Nice? Is that what you call nice—stealing someone's pictures?" I waved my hands in the air. "Well, if that's the kind of friend you want, maybe we shouldn't be friends anymore."

"Maybe we shouldn't." She stormed over to the gate and kicked it open. "So why are you even here?"

"Exactly what I was just wondering." I hurried through the gate. "Good-bye, Emma."

"Good riddance," she snapped, slamming the gate shut behind me.

"Ditto!" I shouted, then turned and sprinted for my house so she wouldn't see me starting to cry.

9

The next couple of weeks were the best and worst of my life. The bad part was mostly Emma, of course. I was trying not to think about our fight, but it wasn't easy. Everything reminded me of her, from our favorite song coming on the radio to a certain shape of cloud floating by over the harbor. Worst of all, though, was that I couldn't seem to stop thinking about what she'd said to me: *There's no law that says I can't have other friends.* I'd never said that, had I? After all, we'd both always had other friends. She did stuff with people from the school band sometimes, and I occasionally hung out with a few of the girls from the swim team. No big deal.

But that was different. We'd always known that those friends weren't *best* friends. That we would always be number one for each other, forever.

Or so I'd thought, anyway. Okay, so maybe she'd been acting a little weird even before our fight. Maybe we hadn't been spending as much time together this summer as usual. Still, I'd known she was there, and that I could always trust her, and that was enough. Only now she wasn't, and I couldn't, and it made me feel like an unmoored boat drifting around at the mercy of the tides, not knowing what would happen next.

Just about the only time I could forget about all that was when I was down at the cove with Admiral Squeak. That was the good part—he was waiting for me almost every time I went down there. I'd practically forgotten that I wasn't supposed to swim without someone else there, racing in to join him whenever I spotted his cute scarred face or his dorsal fin cutting through the still water.

Sometimes we just swam around together enjoying the cool water. Other times he let me hold on to his fin while he dragged me around.

And that wasn't the only trick we practiced. I started bringing along the battered old life preserver Dad had tossed in the shed when he got a new one for the boat, mostly just to give me something to hang on to when I got tired and didn't want to swim back to the shallows. But it wasn't long before Squeak discovered that the floating plastic ring was fun to play with. Sometimes he'd start a lively game of keep-away, while at other times he seemed to enjoy bouncing the ring back and forth between us like a floating game of catch. That gave me an idea, and one day I also brought along an inflatable beach ball and tossed it at him. The first time he just looked surprised when it bounced off his head. But when I giggled and tried again, he seemed to catch on, lifting his head and bumping the ball with his snout.

After a few more sessions, I could convince him to balance it on his nose, at least some of the time.

When I managed to sneak in some computer time, I looked up more tricks. I didn't have a hoop that Squeak could jump through, and I had no idea how to teach him to walk on his tail like the dolphins in the big marine shows. But I learned that dolphins could be trained to respond to hand signals and whistles. I experimented a little and found out that it was true—as soon as Squeak figured out that a certain hand motion meant "please follow," he would do it almost every time! It was pretty cool, and before long, I was sure that Squeak had to be the smartest dolphin ever.

One cloudy Friday morning, I gulped down my breakfast and shot a look into the living room, where Will was sprawled in front of the TV. I tiptoed toward the door, hoping to slip out before he noticed. That was the most challenging part of visiting Squeak. The farther into the summer we got, the more obsessed Jacob became with his scholarship stuff, and the less attention he paid to me and Will. That meant Will was bored a lot of the time, which meant he tried to follow me around whenever he could.

That particular day, he turned and saw me opening the back door. "Where are you going?" he asked, jumping up and skipping into the kitchen.

Holding back a groan, I forced a smile. "Just out," I said. "You wouldn't be interested."

"I don't want to come with you." He hurried over and peered at the clock on the microwave. "Mattie's coming over in, um . . ." I could practically see the little wheels in his brain spinning. "Forty-seven minutes?"

I was surprised, but also relieved. Mattie Ogawa was a year behind Will in school and seemed like a nice enough kid despite having such a snooty older sister. Until that moment, I hadn't even known he and my brother were friends, but I was glad to hear he was coming over. Will didn't have many play dates, and rarely with the same kid twice.

"Okay, have fun," I said, relieved that I wouldn't have to worry about him sneaking down to the cove after me. "Tell Jacob I'll be back in a while."

A cool breeze tickled my face and lifted the short hairs at my temples as I scurried down the rocky trail, grabbing the life preserver and beach ball from behind the bushes halfway down where I'd stashed them yesterday. There were tiny whitecaps on the waves in the cove, and I guessed it wouldn't be long before a summer storm blew in.

Kicking off my shorts and flip-flops, I let out a piercing whistle. A moment later, a familiar gray head popped up halfway out, and I smiled.

Almost an hour later, as Squeak and I rested after a game of tag, I realized I was shivering. The water was the same temperature as ever, but the air must have dropped a good ten degrees since the day before.

"Storm's coming, Squeak," I said, clutching the edge of the life preserver and squinting up at the darkening clouds gathering over the Sound. "Looks like it could be a big one. I'd better go. I might not be able to come down and see you for a day or two if the weather gets bad. But don't give up on me, okay? I'll be back."

Squeak bumped me with his nose, then darted past me, swimming toward shore. I struck out after him, smiling at the way he seemed to read my mind. Had he understood what I'd just said? Or had he sensed the coming storm himself and decided to shoo me out of the water?

Either way, I was amazed and grateful that he'd come into my life, especially now when I really needed a friend. He accompanied me as far into the shallows as he could, letting me rub him all over before swimming off with a flip of his tail.

"See you, Squeak," I murmured, watching him go. Then I turned and waded the rest of the way to shore, shivering again as the cool breeze wrapped itself around me.

The next morning, Saturday, dawned overcast and gusty. It had rained a little overnight, leaving the pines dripping and the ground squishy beneath my feet when I wandered outside to look at the sky.

Mom opened the back door. "Dad just called and said he doubts he'll get many people for lunch service because of the weather," she said. "You kids might as well hang out here at the house unless he needs you. I'm going to run to the grocery store."

"Okay," I said, following her back inside. Jacob and Will were in the living room playing one of their noisy car-driving video games.

Mom bustled around, tucking her keys into her purse and checking her hair in the mirror by the back door. "I'm off," she called to the boys. She glanced at me as she headed for the door. "Stay out of the water today, okay? News says there could be lightning later."

"Sure." She and Dad still didn't know that Emma and I were fighting, which meant they hadn't questioned where I kept disappearing to for hours every day. Any summer before now, I would have been with my best friend.

Maybe I still am, I thought with a secret little smile as I thought about Squeak.

After Mom left, I tried to find something to do. But none of the books or magazines I picked up seemed very interesting, and within moments, the little house felt claustrophobic and dull. I wished I could go over to Emma's like I used to do on stormy days. The big old mansion was full of interesting nooks and crannies to explore, plus there was the Stewart-Bells' full library of videos, a closet stuffed with board games, and the pool table in the basement. Not to mention a best friend who was always coming up with fun ideas . . .

I collapsed onto the sofa, suddenly missing Emma so much I could hardly stand it. Why had I let myself get so worked up over those stupid photos, anyway? Emma was probably right; it had probably all been Morgan's fault. Besides, nobody except me even knew that Squeak was still coming to the cove, so obviously the news story hadn't done any harm . . .

A sudden pounding on the front door interrupted

my thoughts and made me jump. Will looked around from his game.

"Who's that?" he said.

"Must be a delivery or something." Jacob hunched over his controls without looking around. "Nobody else comes to the front door. Can you get it, Annie?"

"Sure." Dragging myself off the couch, I headed through the tiny, rarely-used front parlor and unlatched the front door.

When I swung it open, I was startled to see Morgan Pierce glaring at me. "You stink, Annie Reed!" she yelled.

"Wh-what?" I stammered.

"I heard what you said, and it's so *not* funny!" Her cheeks were red and blotchy. "Seriously, did you think I wouldn't find out? Were you trying to make me mad, or what?"

"What are you talking about?" I clutched the door frame, struck a little off-balance by her attack. *I* was supposed to be mad at *her*, not the other way around. After all, she was the one who'd stolen my best friend. Hearing a muffled giggle, I noticed for the first time that Grace Ogawa was standing a little behind Morgan, half hidden by an overgrown shrub.

My attention snapped back to Morgan as she crossed her arms over her chest. "You *know* what I'm talking about," she spat out. "My father is a pillar of this community, you know. If you have a problem with me, take it up with me; don't make fun of him. He doesn't deserve that!"

I got a little stuck on "pillar of this community"—it was such a Morgan thing to say—and it took me a second to realize what she had to be talking about. When I did, I gulped.

"Oh," I said. "Um, the name . . ."

"Admiral Squeak?!" she exclaimed. "Really? You're seriously obnoxious enough to make fun of my dad's scar like that? Talk about juvenile! Well, you're going to regret being such a jerk, Annie Reed. Trust me!"

Turning on her heel, she grabbed Grace by the arm and stomped away.

10

All I could do for a moment was stand there staring after Morgan. When she disappeared around the corner of the road, I finally blinked and staggered back, pushing the door shut and then collapsing against it.

At first, all I felt was a vague sense of guilt. I hoped Morgan hadn't told Admiral Zeke about the nickname. She was right; he didn't deserve that, and I hated the thought that he might think I was making fun of his scar. After all, I'd spent a lifetime hating the way people reacted to my brother's missing fingers—as if it made him incomplete, weird, different from normal people in some important way. Did the admiral feel like that about his scar? I'd never really thought about it before.

I also couldn't help feeling a little nervous. Morgan had a scary temper, and she was definitely the type of person to hold a grudge. Even if she never said a word about this to her father, she'd make sure I paid. I could count on that.

Maybe I should try to find her, see if she'll let me apologize, I thought. *She's probably over at Emma's right now . . .*

Thinking of Emma suddenly chased all the other feelings out of me, to be replaced by growing fury. I clenched my fists as I realized what this meant.

"She told her," I murmured. "I can't believe she actually *told* her!"

This had to be Emma's fault. Nobody else outside my family and Will's two friends knew about that nickname. And now that we weren't speaking, there was nothing stopping my former best friend from spilling all my secrets to my worst enemy.

Former best friend. The words made me feel lonely and confused, and my anger faded away as quickly as it had come. Glancing out the window, I thought about running down to the cove. Squeak was the only one who might be able to make me feel better right now.

A sudden gust of wind rattled the window, and I shivered. This wasn't a good time to be down by the water. I'd just have to wait to see Squeak.

I wandered back into the main part of the house. Jacob heard me come in and looked around.

"Who was at the door?" he asked.

"Nobody," I said. "Just someone, uh, looking for directions."

Jacob glanced at the window as another gust swooped down around the house. "I'd hate to be lost out in this weather," he said. "It's probably going to start pouring any second." He stood and stretched. "Better get my work done on the computer in case the power goes out later. Keep an eye on you-know-who, okay?" He ruffled Will's hair on his way past.

"Don't worry, I'll keep an eye on her," Will said with a grin.

As soon as our older brother had disappeared up the stairs, Will dropped the video game controls and loped over to me. He pressed his face up against my arm.

"Stop it—what are you doing?" I shoved him away.

He pushed his face at me again, giggling. "I'm keeping an *eye* on you," he said. "Get it? My eye's *on* you."

"Ha-ha, very funny," I said limply. "Why don't you go back to your game, okay?"

"I'm tired of it. Let's play hide-and-seek."

Before I could respond, the phone rang over on the kitchen counter. I hurried over and grabbed it. "Hello, Reed residence," I said.

"Hi, this is Mattie Ogawa," a child's voice said. "Is Will there?"

"Sure, hang on." I was surprised. Will rarely got phone calls from anyone except our grandma in Florida. Had he finally found a real friend? "Will, it's for you," I said, holding the receiver out to my brother. "It's Mattie."

Will grabbed the phone. "Hello? Is this really Mattie?" He listened for a moment, then shot me a sidelong look and scurried around the corner into the parlor.

I rolled my eyes, wondering what made him think I wanted to listen to his stupid little-kid conversation. Especially now, when I needed to figure out what to do about this whole Morgan situation.

Flopping onto the couch, I stared at the ceiling without really seeing it. What could I do to stop Morgan from being mad?

Nothing, I realized. And why should I care, anyway? That nickname wasn't meant as an insult. And it was Will who came up with it anyway, not me.

For a second, I considered trying to tell Morgan that. Everyone on the Point knew that Will was—well, kind of special. Even Morgan couldn't hold something like this against him, could she?

I banished the idea almost as soon as it came. Why bother? Morgan was completely unreasonable. And if she was going to take it out on anyone, it should be me, not my little brother.

Anyway, I'm not scared of her, I thought, playing with a frayed thread sticking out of the couch. *What's she going to do to me?*

I tried not to imagine too many possible answers to that question. Sitting up, I glanced toward the window. The sky looked a little lighter—maybe I could sneak in a trip to the cove before Mom got home after all.

Just then, Will ran back into the room. He tossed the phone receiver at the base and missed, sending it clattering across the counter.

"Oops," he said.

I just rolled my eyes and went over to put it back properly. "What'd Mattie want?" I asked.

"Nothing!" Will shouted. "Nothing at all, nope, nothing. Absolutely nada."

"Okay." I wondered if he'd sneaked some of Jacob's energy bars that morning. He was acting like he did when he had too much sugar—extra hyper and jumpy. "Listen, I have to go out for a while, okay?"

"You do?" He ran over and grabbed me by the arm. "No! Don't go, Annie. Stay here with me!"

I shook him off, trying not to let my irritation show. "Jacob!" I yelled up the stairs. "I'm going out. Be back in a bit."

He appeared at the top of the steps. "What? Now? Where?" he asked.

"I'll be back soon. See you!" I hurried out before he could ask any more questions or tell me not to go, closing the door on the sound of Will's wail of protest.

All the way to the cove trail, I kept expecting Will to run up behind me. But Jacob must have convinced him to stay inside, because he didn't come.

I glanced at the sky as I started down the steep path. Clouds still scudded overhead, dark and dreary. But it hadn't started raining yet, and the wind seemed to be dying down a little. Maybe the storm wouldn't hit us after all.

Down at the beach, I whistled loudly several times, but Squeak didn't appear. I paced back and forth, wishing I'd thought to put on my swimsuit. Then again, maybe it was better that I couldn't be tempted into the water. On a stormy day like this, there could be dangerous currents out there. I was a strong swimmer, but even I didn't want to get caught in a riptide or something.

Besides, Squeak didn't seem to be in the cove anyway. I perched on an only-slightly-damp rock near the tidal pool, staring out at the white-capped waves. I'd expected the dolphin to be tucked into some corner of the cove hiding out from the storm, but if he was here, I was sure he would have responded to my calls. Where could he be?

An hour later, it started to sprinkle and I finally gave up. I hurried up the trail, squinting against the increasing rain. At the top of the cliff, I broke into a run, bursting into the house just as thunder rumbled in the distance.

When I entered, Will leaped up off the couch as if he had ants in his pants. "Annie!" he shouted. "Where were you?"

"Nowhere." I pushed a damp lock of hair off my face. "I'm going to change."

Will followed me all the way to my room, lurking outside the door as I pulled on a dry pair of shorts and my favorite swim team tee. When I came out, he was dancing from foot to foot.

"What's with you today?" I grumbled, pushing past him on my way to the bathroom. Once again, he hung out in the hall until I finished, padding downstairs after me. I sighed, doing my best to ignore him and hoping Mom got home soon.

Half an hour later, I gave up trying to read and tossed my book aside. "Want some lunch?" I asked Will. "We might as well not wait for Mom—she probably stopped by the restaurant on her way home from the store or something."

"I have to tell you something," Will blurted out.

I headed for the pantry and grabbed a loaf of bread. "First tell me if you want tuna or PB and J."

"No, listen!" He grabbed my arm, almost making me drop the bread. "It's about Admiral Squeak."

That got my attention. "What about him?"

"Morgan found out about his name. She's really mad." Will flapped his hands anxiously. "She said she's going to get revenge."

I tossed the bread onto the counter. "What do you mean, get revenge?" I said. "Revenge on who?"

"Like I said! Admiral Squeak!" He sounded frustrated. "She and her friends are going out on Jet Skis to find him! They're going to chase him out of the cove and the harbor and make sure he never comes back!"

"What?" I grabbed him by the shoulders. "Will, what are you talking about? How could you possibly know that?"

Before he even spoke, the answer came to me: Mattie.

Grace Ogawa was one of Morgan's best friends. Mattie must have overheard them talking and told his new friend Will.

"Will, what else did Mattie say?" I shook him, feeling frantic. "When are they going?"

"At noon." Will squirmed out of my grip, reaching up to rub his shoulder where I'd squeezed it. "I was going to tell you before, but you were being mean so I didn't."

I spun around to look at the clock on the microwave. It read 12:48.

"Oh no!" I moaned. "I have to stop them! Stay here."

I guess I sounded pretty serious, because Will didn't argue and just watched silently as I yanked on my sneakers and crashed out of the house.

Outside, I grabbed my bike from the shed and flung myself onto it, thanking my lucky stars that the rain had stopped again, at least for the moment. I pumped hard, skidding around the curve onto the road leading down into town.

My head was throbbing with fear. Would even the horrible Morgan Pierce really take out her anger on a helpless animal? I wasn't sure. But I couldn't take the chance. I was the one who'd convinced Squeak to trust me—to think people were friends. It would be my fault if something terrible happened to him because of that.

The marina was mostly deserted—no surprise, given the weather. Nobody was crazy enough to risk their boat—or their life—heading out into an oncoming storm. Or were they? Squinting through the salty spray whipped up by the wind, I tried to guess which Jet Skis belonged to Connor and his buddies. Had the storm convinced them not to go after all?

But I couldn't count on that, and I had no way of knowing which Jet Skis were which. I shivered as another gust almost knocked me over and thunder rumbled somewhere out over the Sound. If my parents knew I was even this close to the water on a day like today, they'd kill me. But I had to help Squeak. He trusted me, and I couldn't let him down no matter what. Dropping my bike on the dock, I jumped into my family's fishing boat and scrabbled under the seat cushion for the key Dad always hid there.

My hands shook as I untied the boat, then inserted the key into the ignition. Taking a deep breath, I turned the key, and the engine roared to life.

11

I kept the boat slow as I steered out of the marina. The water was choppier than usual due to the stormy weather, and the rain was starting up again, tiny droplets stinging my face and making it hard to see. I hunched over the wheel, peering forward and trying not to hit anything. I realized I'd forgotten to put on a life jacket, but I didn't dare take my hands off the wheel to grab one from under the seat.

When I reached open water, I opened up the throttle a little bit. The steering wheel jerked and jumped in my hand as the hull hit an especially big wave, and I felt the boat shudder.

Swallowing hard, I blinked rainwater out of my eyes, clamped down more tightly on the wheel, and let up a little on the acceleration. I'd driven the boat lots of times—well, mostly our old boat, which was even bigger—but never without Dad right there to help. I was going to have to pay attention if I didn't want to mess up.

Soon I'd left the marina behind. A few larger yachts and sailboats were anchored out in the middle of the harbor, but it was easy to steer around those. Then the fishing boat was pointed straight toward Little Twin Cove.

But I'm probably getting all worked up for nothing, I told myself. *Squeak wasn't even there earlier.*

That was true. But Morgan and the others didn't know that. They'd probably look for him there first, especially if Emma told them she'd seen him there more than once.

My grip tightened on the wheel again at the thought of Emma's betrayal. How could she have told Morgan about that stupid nickname? It was bad enough that she was ignoring me, but I never would have expected her to do something that could hurt an innocent creature. Or to break a promise, for that matter, even if we weren't friends anymore.

Catching a flash of movement out of the corner of my eye, I turned my head, Squeak's name already on my lips. But no—it wasn't him. Just chaotic whitecaps tossed up by the wind.

When I got closer to the cove, I heard a new sound over the moan of the wind—motors. Peering through the misty rain-spattered air, I spotted several Jet Skis up ahead.

The drivers saw me, too. All three of the Jet Skis turned and raced toward my boat. When they neared, I recognized Connor and two of his equally obnoxious friends. A girl clung on behind each boy. Morgan was riding with Connor, and Grace Ogawa was hanging on to the second boy. The third girl was Emma.

I gritted my teeth, glaring at her. But it was Morgan who shouted my name.

"Annie! What took you so long?" she yelled, sounding annoyed. "We were about to go back in."

I pushed a chunk of wet hair out of my eyes. "What are you talking about?" I shouted back. "Will told me what you said, and I won't let you do it!"

"Duh, him telling you was the whole point," Grace said, tossing her wet black ponytail back over her shoulder. She glanced over at Morgan. "Told you she wouldn't follow the plan."

"Ems said she'd come running right over," Morgan called back, shifting her glare to Emma. "How was I supposed to know she'd mess it up?"

Hold on. What was going on here? "What plan?" I snapped, grabbing the wheel for balance as an especially big swell rolled the boat from side to side. "Will told me—"

"Yeah, yeah, like Grace said, that was the whole point," Morgan exclaimed with a scowl. "Her brat of a brother was supposed to spill the beans to your spaz of a brother. And everyone knows *he* can't keep his mouth shut."

"So he was supposed to tell me," I said, feeling stupid as I finally figured out what was happening here. They'd set me up! Or tried to, anyway. Leave it to Will to actually keep a secret for once in his life.

"Yeah." Grace giggled loudly. "We figured you'd go storming over to Morgan's house right away, and we'd be waiting for you there." She loosened her grip on the boy in front of her just long enough to make a snip-snip scissors motion with her fingers, pretending to cut her ponytail.

I gasped as Morgan, Grace, and the boys laughed. Had they really planned to grab me and cut off my hair? Even for Morgan, that seemed crazy mean. Could she really be *that* mad about some stupid nickname?

Shooting a look at Emma, I saw that she looked kind of ill. Good. She deserved a little seasickness after the way she'd betrayed me—over and over again.

"Anyway, when you didn't show up we were afraid you might be just as big a spaz as your brother," Morgan said. "We talked the guys into coming out to see if you were actually out here looking for that stupid dolphin."

Connor revved his motor. "Yeah, and I'm ready to go back," he said. "This rain's a drag. Plus my dad'll kill me if he finds out I went out in this storm."

The other two boys revved their motors, too. I slumped in my seat, relieved that they were leaving. In fact, now that I thought about it, I realized they'd never intended to harass Squeak at all—just me. That made me feel a tiny bit better, though not much.

"Hey, watch it," I cried as one of the boys zoomed past the boat, so close that his wake washed up over the side.

It was the Jet Ski that Grace was riding, and she glanced back at me and laughed. "Do it again!" she urged the guy.

Meanwhile, Connor and the other boy were following their friend's lead. Soon all three Jet Skis were zooming around in circles, coming as close to my boat as they dared.

"Stop it!" Emma cried, sounding terrified. "You'll hit her!"

"No we won't." Connor cackled. "I'd never do that to my Jet Ski."

"Oh yeah? I might!" The guy with Grace revved his motor again and zoomed straight toward the side of my boat, peeling off at the last second and sending another wash of seawater over the side.

"Quit that!" I yelled, swiping the moisture off my face. I was soaked to the skin by then, but I hardly noticed. I was too busy trying to start the engine up again.

Finally it roared to life. I spun the wheel, trying to turn back toward the marina, but Connor was there in front of me, zipping back and forth. I had to turn to the side to avoid him, and then turn again when the kid with Emma zoomed up to cut off my path.

"Get out of my way!" I yelled over the increasing clamor of the wind and rain. The storm was finally coming for real, and I definitely wanted to get back on dry land before it arrived in full force.

They ignored me, Morgan and Grace egging the boys on and all of them laughing as they herded me farther and farther from the marina. Well, almost all of them. Emma wasn't laughing, or saying anything at all. She was hanging on tightly to the boy in front of her, her face a mask of fear.

But I barely noticed that as I struggled to get the boat back on course. We were getting awfully close to the mouth of the harbor—and the rough, storm-tossed waters of the Sound beyond. My heart pounded as I tried not to imagine what would happen to my little boat out there in this kind of weather.

Connor—I was pretty sure it was him, though it was raining harder now, making it difficult to see—roared toward me again.

"Oh no!" he yelled over the wailing wind. "My steering's gone—I'm going to crash!"

With a little scream, I yanked the wheel hard to one side, cutting the motor at the same time. Bracing for impact, I was relieved when the Jet Ski veered off at the last second—until I heard Connor hooting with laughter.

That rat! He'd tricked me again. Gritting my teeth, I grabbed the key and jerked it, but nothing happened. Stupid boat! I tried again and again.

"See you, loser!" Morgan shouted. "Remember this the next time you think about messing with my family!"

The wind grabbed her shriek of laughter, whipping it away as Connor turned and roared off in the direction of the marina. The other two Jet Skis followed. I squinted through the rain, watching them go. It looked like Emma was turning around to stare at me, but it was raining pretty hard and I couldn't be sure.

"Good riddance," I muttered, trying again to start the engine. All I got in return was an ominous clicking sound.

I gulped, suddenly remembering what Dad had told me about this boat: *Her engine's a little older and more temperamental than our other boat. You don't want to flood it.*

"Oh no," I cried, panic zipping through me like an electric shock. "No, no, no!" I tried again, turning the key more gently this time, but it was no use. The engine was flooded, and I had no idea how to fix it.

A large wave hit us square in the side, almost tossing me out of the driver's seat. I gripped the wheel with trembling hands, trying to figure out what to do. Were there even any oars on this thing? Maybe I could paddle back to shore.

Glancing over my shoulder, I gulped as I saw Long Island Sound looming just beyond the mouth of the harbor. It might as well have been the Atlantic—I couldn't catch even the slightest glimpse of the New York side, not in this kind of weather. All the stories I'd ever heard around town about people lost at sea danced through my head, making me feel hot and cold all at once, wishing I could turn back time to before I'd flooded the engine, or maybe before I'd decided to rush out here in the boat at all. After all, it turned out Squeak had never even been in any danger—but now I was, for sure. What was I going to do?

Another huge wave crashed up over the side of the boat, spray mixing with the rain. Several inches of water were sloshing around in the bottom by now, and I realized I'd better bail out if I didn't want to capsize.

Having something to do distracted me—at least a little bit—from my terror. I yanked open a cupboard, grabbed the bucket stowed there, and got to work. But the faster I bailed, the faster the storm dumped more water in the boat. Worse yet, when I paused for a rest, I could see that I was moving even more rapidly out toward the Sound!

"No, no, no!" I muttered as the panic took hold again. There was no way the boat could stay afloat if it ended up out there . . .

CRASH! This time the wave was so big it knocked me into the side of the boat. I hung on as the boat spun around crazily, one side tipping dangerously close to the surface. I gasped for breath, then choked as water—rain, sea, or both—splashed into my mouth and down my throat.

Coughing and shoving wet hair out of my eyes, I crawled over to another cabinet. This one held several bright orange life jackets. Pulling one out, I yanked it on over my T-shirt and snapped the buckles with shaking, fumbling fingers.

I was just in time. The next wave washed all the way over the boat, leaving behind way too much water. My whole body started shaking as the boat foundered, the bow dipping below the surface.

Half lunging and half swimming over to the starboard side, I shoved myself over the edge and pushed off, striking out away from the boat. I'd heard of people getting sucked underwater by a capsizing boat and didn't want to take any chances.

Seconds later, the fishing boat had disappeared beneath the waves. I bobbed there, trying to blink the rain and salt spray out of my eyes, glad for the life jacket helping to keep me afloat in the rough water.

I couldn't believe this was happening to me. I'd been raised on the water; I knew the rules. This sort of thing only happened to other people—like the stupid tourists who didn't pay attention to weather warnings and had to be rescued by the Coast Guard.

So where was the Coast Guard now? *They have no idea I'm out here*, I realized, my heart clenching into a cold, hard knot of fear in my chest as I pictured the fishing boat's radio—now lost beneath the churning sea. *Nobody does. Nobody except people who hate me.*

I tried to tell myself that Emma might not be totally hopeless—that she might tell someone I was out here. After all, she'd always been a worrier. Then again, why would she be worried now? The last time she'd seen me, I'd still had the boat. She and Morgan and Grace were probably back at the Cottage giggling over hot cocoa by now, making fun of the way I'd rushed out to save Squeak.

The thought made me want to cry, but I didn't have the energy to waste on that. If nobody was coming to save me, I'd have to save myself. Spinning around, I squinted at the horizon, trying to figure out which direction to swim. The marina seemed impossibly far away, but I didn't think I'd gone that far past the cove. Maybe I could make it back there on my own.

Catching a glimpse of something I thought might be the Point, I struck out that way, my arms windmilling wildly. It was hard to perform a proper crawl stroke with the life jacket on, but I did my best. Pull, pull, kick, kick—the familiar movements should have come easily. But the harbor's rough waters felt foreign, nothing at all like the school pool or the quiet cove. I'd always been at home in the water, any water, but this time it was my enemy, fighting me and sapping my energy with every stroke. Before long, my arms and legs felt heavy and slow.

I can do this, I told myself. *I'm one of the best swimmers on the team. Coach even said I might make states next year.*

That kept me going for another dozen strokes or so. Then a wave washed over me, leaving me with a mouth full of salt water. Spitting it out, I stopped swimming just long enough to shove the hair out of my eyes. I looked around again, but this time I couldn't see the shore at all—the rain was coming down too hard.

I floated there for a moment, not sure what to do. It wouldn't do me any good to swim in the wrong direction. That could send me out to the Sound at worst, or leave me floundering around aimlessly until I ran out of energy. And I already felt so exhausted I could barely lift my arm to rub my eyes.

Leaning back against the support of the life jacket, I let myself float and rest. *Dead man's float*, I thought, my eyes drifting shut. *Now I understand why they call it that. Or is that only when you're floating facedown? I can't remember . . .*

I was a little surprised to realize that I wasn't that scared anymore. That seemed weird, but I couldn't quite focus on figuring it out. My mind felt jumbled, and my limbs seemed filled with lead. It was tempting to give up, let myself float along to wherever the current took me. What else could I do after all? Maybe I'd end up across the Sound on the North Shore of Long Island. Or maybe I'd float all the way down to Florida, where my family had gone once on vacation to visit my grandma.

I was thinking about that trip, the way the water in the lagoon where we'd gone snorkeling was so clear you could see straight to the bottom, when I felt something bump my leg. A second later, a gray dorsal fin broke the surface right in front of me.

My entire body pulsed with terror, certain that a shark had come to finish me off. But a familiar face appeared, the jagged scar apparent even through the driving rain.

"Squeak!" I cried, then coughed, almost choking on the wave that splashed into my mouth. Another wave washed over me, along with hope and sudden joy. Squeak had come! Nobody else knew I was in trouble, but he'd sensed it and he'd come. I'd known he was special, and this proved it.

The dolphin swam closer, pressing up against me. I grabbed for him, my nearly numb fingers clasping his dorsal fin. It felt so familiar that I almost laughed. Who knew our games would come to this? Letting out a chirp, Squeak swam off.

I held on for a few seconds, then felt my grip slipping. "No!" I cried as I spun away from the dolphin.

He was back at my side in a second, pushing against me, whistling and nudging me with his snout. Once again, I grabbed hold, this time using both hands. And once again, he swam off into the storm. Did he know where he was going? I had no idea, but I was too busy holding on to worry about it.

The next few minutes passed in a daze. But I woke up a little when the rain slowed a bit and the familiar shape of the Point loomed up before me, closer than I might have expected. Squeak was bringing me back to the cove!

That gave me extra energy to grip even more

tightly to his fin. "Go, Squeak, go!" I shouted over the storm.

Then another sound broke through the din of wind and rain—a motor. The first I'd heard since . . . Oh no! My heart pounded with fear. Had Morgan and the others come back?

But it wasn't Jet Skis coming toward me. A much larger shape loomed—a yacht, the searchlight on its bow sweeping the waves.

"There!" someone yelled, a man's voice faint in the distance. "Is that her?"

"Dad?" I blinked and peered through the rain. "Daddy?"

"It's her!" someone else shouted, even though it was impossible that anyone could have heard me over the storm. "Quick, the ring!"

The yacht slowed as it neared me, and a moment later, something slapped the water a dozen yards away. It was a bright orange rescue ring on a long rope. Using my last few shreds of strength I lunged toward it, losing my grip on Squeak's fin.

"Grab it, Annie!" someone—my dad?—shouted.

I opened my mouth to reply but ended up gulping down more seawater. I choked, trying to catch my breath, staring at the ring bobbing there an impossible distance away. *So close and yet so far*, I thought, trying to remember where that saying came from as another wave washed over me, taking me by surprise and filling my nose and mouth once again. Losing my sense of up and down in the swirling water, I tried to take a breath but choked and realized I was underwater.

Then something bumped me hard from below. Squeak! He surfaced, half lifting me along with him. My hands grabbed at him, sliding over his smooth, wet skin. He chirped as I finally found his dorsal fin again, clutching it as tightly as I could.

"Look!" someone on the yacht yelled. "Is that a dolphin?"

This time I didn't bother trying to respond, focusing on hanging on. "The ring, Squeak," I mumbled. "Get the ring."

I wasn't sure if he'd understand the word, even though he'd probably heard it a hundred times as we were playing with that battered old ring in the cove. Would he take me toward the boat, or continue on our way back to the cove? Either way, I trusted him to keep me safe. He was my friend, and he'd never let me down before.

The dolphin let out his special signature whistle as I scrabbled for a better hold on his fin. Then he started swimming—right toward the rescue ring! I smiled. *The smartest dolphin in the world . . .* I thought proudly. Soon I was able to let go of him and grab the ring.

"Thanks, Squeak," I whispered as he slipped back underwater. Blinking the moisture out of my eyes, I peered through the sheets of rain, wanting one last glimpse of the dolphin who'd saved my life. Was that his tail over there, flapping at me as he dove beneath the storm-tossed waves? I wasn't sure, but was too tired to do anything but hang on as Dad and the others dragged me toward the yacht.

12

An hour later, I was wrapped in a scratchy but warm wool blanket, sitting in front of the restaurant's huge stove. Dad had turned on all the burners and lit the oven, leaving the door open to allow warm, dry heat to pour out over me. Even so, I couldn't seem to stop shivering.

"Are you sure we shouldn't take her to the emergency room?" Mom fretted, bustling over to lay the back of her hand against my forehead. "Annie, do you know what day it is?"

"Still Saturday," I said. "Just like the last fifteen times you asked."

Will spun wildly across the room. Jacob stepped forward and grabbed him before he could crash into the hot stove.

"Did Admiral Squeak really save you, Annie?" Will exclaimed.

I shot a look at Admiral Zeke, who was over near the doorway talking to my dad, Emma's mom, and several other people. Had he heard Will use that silly nickname? I hoped not, but couldn't really find it in me to care very much.

"He did," I told Will with a small smile. "And you did, too."

Will grinned, looking bashful all of a sudden. Had my comment actually rendered him speechless? Well, that was okay—it was true. As soon as Mom had walked in from shopping, Will had told her everything. She'd called Emma's mom, who had no idea what was going on, and then Dad. He'd raced out to the boat to look for me, only to find it missing. Since he'd run off in too much of a hurry to remember his phone, he'd run into the yacht club's clubhouse to use theirs. Admiral Zeke had just been coming out and asked what was wrong—and while Dad was telling him, Morgan and the others had roared into the marina on their Jet Skis. Not even Morgan messed around with her dad, and soon she and her friends admitted what they'd done—and Admiral Zeke had insisted on taking Dad out to search for me in his fancy zillion dollar yacht.

"I'm glad you didn't wash away out to sea," Will told me solemnly. "I'd miss you."

"I'd miss you, too, Will." Snaking one arm out from under the blanket, I squeezed his hand.

Out of the corner of my eye, I saw someone creeping toward me. It was Emma—she'd been there when Dad and the admiral and I came in a little while ago, along with her mother and the rest of my family, though I hadn't spoken to her or even really looked at her.

"Annie?" she said softly. "Can I, um, talk to you?"

I glanced at Will. "Why don't you go check on Dad, okay?"

"Um . . ." He shuffled his feet, shooting Emma an uncertain glance. But then he hurried off without arguing.

"Okay." I took a deep breath, looking directly at Emma for the first time. "Talk."

"I'm really sorry about what happened," she said all in a rush. "Seriously, Annie, I mean it—I had no idea what they were planning, and then before I knew it, we were rushing out on the Jet Skis, and, well, I just thought they wanted to chase the dolphin around a little, and I figured we'd never be able to find him anyway, so it didn't matter. By the time they told me the real plan, it was too late." She tugged on her new, shorter hair. "I never would've done what they said," she added softly.

"Yeah right." I might have fallen for their lies before, but I wasn't stupid enough to do it again.

"Like you didn't know about the hair cutting? Give me a break, Emma."

"I didn't!" she cried. "I swear!"

I rolled my eyes. "Just like you didn't tell Morgan about the whole Admiral Squeak thing, right?"

"Huh?" She shook her head. "I already told you she saw those pictures by accident."

"Okay. So was it an accident when you told her we named him after her dad, too?" My voice dripped with sarcasm, and I expected her to get mad.

But she just looked confused. "I didn't tell her that," she said. "Come to think of it, I'm not sure how she found out."

I stared at her. Emma had never been much of an actress—she just didn't have it in her to hide her true feelings most of the time. But right now she was ready for an Academy Award.

Will sidled closer, and I realized he'd never really left—just moved away a little bit. "Annie?"

he said in a funny little voice. "Don't blame Emma. It was me. I told her."

"What?" I turned to stare at him. "What did you say? Told who what?"

He took a deep breath, looking uncharacteristically solemn. "I guess I told Morgan. Only I really just told Mattie, but his sister was there, too, and she might've told Morgan, right?"

My eyes widened, and I glanced at Emma, who was nodding slowly. So that was what had happened. Will hadn't been able to resist bragging to his new friend about the cool dolphin he'd seen— and named. And all it had taken was for Grace to hear it, and, well . . .

"I'm sorry." Will's lower lip quivered. "Do you forgive me, Annie?"

"Of course." I pulled him closer and hugged him. His wiry body felt warm and wiggly in my arms, and after a few seconds, he pulled free and ran across the kitchen, already moving on to the next thing.

As I watched him go, Emma cleared her throat. "What about me?" she asked softly. "Do you forgive me, Annie? Because I'm really sorry. About—about everything."

I looked at her, not sure what to say. I was glad to know that she really hadn't purposely betrayed me. Not about the dolphin's name, anyway. But did I forgive her for the rest? For becoming friends with Morgan, for cutting her hair, for letting everything change? I wasn't sure, and right now I was too tired to think about it.

"I don't know," I said with a yawn. "But can we talk about it later? I think I might need a nap. For about a year."

A few weeks later, I sat on the rocky beach of Little Twin, arms wrapped around my legs and chin resting on my knees, staring out at the calm water. It was a warm day, but with a cool breeze that wouldn't quite let me forget that school started in less than a week and winter would be coming soon after that. Where had the summer gone?

My eyes scanned the cove, searching for a dorsal fin, a familiar scarred face. But all I saw were a few gulls wheeling around in the sky and a tiny crab scuttling across the sand.

I'd seen quite a bit of Squeak for a week or so after the storm. He'd greeted me there at the cove almost every time I showed up, just like before.

But then he'd skipped a day. And then two days. Over the past couple of weeks, his visits had become less and less frequent, and now I hadn't seen him in four whole days.

I tried to tell myself it was no surprise. The first couple of days after the storm, Mom hadn't let me out of her sight, and I'd used the time to study up on dolphins some more—especially since my whole family was pretty much doing whatever I said, which included Jacob letting me use the computer as much as I wanted. Mom and Dad hadn't even punished me for taking the boat out by myself and letting it capsize. Well, not much, anyway. Dad had said something about me working extra shifts at the restaurant to help pay the insurance deductible. Mostly my parents made me promise to never, ever do something like that again.

Anyway, all my extra reading had told me that Squeak was likely to move south to warmer waters soon. If he hadn't left already . . .

I sighed, my eyes sweeping the cove again. If only I'd known the last time I'd seen him could be it, I at least would have said good-bye.

"Hey!" a voice rang out, breaking through my gloomy thoughts.

Sitting up straight, I saw Zoe hurrying down the steep cove trail. I smiled and waved.

"You're late," I said as I stood up to meet her.

"Sorry," she said breathlessly, flinging the backpack she was carrying down beside the cooler I'd hauled with me. "But I just texted the others, and they'll be here soon. They're bringing the rest of the food."

"Cool." Zoe and I had been spending more and more time together lately. As it turned out, none of the bad stuff Morgan had said about her was true. She hadn't been kicked out of her last school, and her mother wasn't a flake, either. She did travel a lot, but only because she helped start and run charities all over the world.

"Want a soda?" Zoe zipped open her backpack. "I just took them out of the fridge, so they're still cold."

"Sure, thanks." I stepped over to the cooler and opened it. "I brought hot dog buns and Dad's portable grill."

Zoe handed me a cold can of soda. Then she pushed up her glasses, shooting me a sidelong look. "Actually, the reason I was late is because I ran into Morgan and Emma on my way here."

"Really?" I fiddled with pull tab of my soda, trying not to sound too interested. Emma had stopped by the day after the storm, and we'd talked a little. She'd started to apologize again, but then Will had run in wanting to tell us about some bird he'd just seen eating a lizard, and she'd left pretty soon after that. I hadn't heard from her since.

"Yeah," Zoe told me. "I invited them to the cookout, and they said they might stop by."

I knew what that meant. Sadness washed through me as I realized things really had changed this summer. But maybe I'd get used to it. Maybe I already had. Like my dad always said, nothing really ever stayed the same, whether in the ocean or anywhere else. Right?

A chatter of excited voices burst out overhead, and Zoe and I looked up. The other girls were coming. Abby and Kayla were from my swim team; I'd known them for years, though I'd never really hung out with them much before Zoe came along. The third girl, Rebecca, was a year behind us in school and didn't swim—she couldn't, since she wore braces on her legs and used a cane. But Zoe had

180

met her at the yacht club and it turned out she was hilarious and knew just about everything there was to know about anything fun. I couldn't believe she'd been right there in my town all these years and I'd never even talked to her.

"Hi!" I called out as the other two girls helped Rebecca maneuver down the steep trail. "I thought you guys would never get here."

They laughed and started chattering about the long line at the grocery store where they'd stopped on their way here. Zoe joined in with gusto. I barely said a word, just enjoying their friendly energy. Having a best friend was great, but it was nice to be part of a group, too. Not the same, but nice.

Half an hour later, the hot dogs were sizzling on the grill and we were sitting on the picnic blanket Zoe had brought, sipping soda and eating chips and carrot sticks and Marta the nanny's homemade macaroons.

"So, Annie." Kayla shot me a mischievous look. "Should we be, like, super honored that a TV star like you is hanging out with a bunch of nobodies like the rest of us?"

"Stop." I leaned over and gave her a shove while everyone laughed.

"Seriously, though." Rebecca selected a chip. "How ridiculous was that story? Morgan's mom totally made it all about her heroic husband rushing off to the rescue."

"Yeah." Zoe rolled her eyes. "And conveniently forgot to mention it was her own bratty daughter who caused the whole thing."

I picked at my food, forcing a smile. Mrs. Pierce had insisted on featuring the story of me being rescued by Squeak and her husband on her show, then made me look like a total idiot who'd cluelessly decided to go boating during a huge storm. Everyone else told me it hadn't been that bad, but it still bugged me.

But I was trying to forget about it. After all, everyone I cared about knew what had really happened.

Besides, some real good had come out of that story. Morgan's mom had mentioned Dad's restaurant by name a couple of times. And ever since the show had aired, we'd been so busy that we had to turn away as many customers as we served. They came from everywhere—not just New Haven and New London, but lots from New York City and Providence and Boston and even farther away. Especially after a famous restaurant reviewer came the week after the storm and wrote a glowing article about Dad's seafood stew. It was framed and hanging by the register where everyone could see it, along with several photos of Squeak. Dad had asked me for some, since customers were always asking about the dolphin they'd seen on the news. They weren't the pictures Emma had taken—those were from too far away, and besides, everyone thought Morgan had taken them. I'd snapped some new ones of Squeak playing in the shallows a few days after the storm when Mom had finally let me visit him again.

Anyway, Dad was already talking about expanding into the vacant building next door, though Mom insisted he wait a while to see if business died down again once people forgot about that TV show. I was pretty sure it wouldn't die down much, though. Once people tasted Dad's food, they tended to come back again and again.

"Hey!" Zoe said suddenly, poking me in the shoulder. "Look who's here!"

I glanced first toward the trail, expecting—hoping?—to see Emma coming to join us after all. But my other friends were all staring out toward the water. When I followed their gaze, my heart skipped. It was Squeak!

The dolphin was swimming back and forth in the deep water, occasionally leaping out and splashing down again. "Excuse me," I said, jumping up and peeling off my shorts. We'd planned to go swimming later—we wanted to get in as much fun in the water as we could before school started—so I had my swimsuit on underneath.

Soon I was splashing out to meet my dolphin friend. Squeak rushed to greet me, letting out his familiar little whistle-chirp as he bumped me with his nose.

"Hey, buddy," I said, rubbing him all over. "I thought you might not be coming back. But I'm really glad you did."

Suddenly I heard another whistle from off to one side. My eyes widened as another dolphin surfaced a few yards away—and another, and another. It was hard to count the sleek gray bodies leaping and swimming around over there, but I was pretty sure there were at least half a dozen of them.

"Squeak!" I exclaimed. "Is that your pod?"

Squeak chirped, then pulled away, swimming toward the other dolphins. Halfway there, he stopped and turned around, gliding back to me. Letting out another soft chirp, he rubbed against me, almost knocking me over.

I laughed and patted him, tears coming to my eyes as I realized what came next. "Good-bye,

Squeak," I said, rubbing his beautiful scarred face. "Thanks for coming to see me before you go."

He nuzzled me one last time, then spun around and leaped out of the water, heading toward the rest of the pod. They whistled in greeting as he reached them, and the whole group swam off in the direction of the harbor.

"Good-bye, friend," I whispered, not taking my eyes off the graceful gray forms leaping and dancing through the waves. "Good-bye."

I kept my eyes on the water, still searching the horizon for the dolphins long after they'd disappeared. Would Squeak come back next summer? Or was he gone for good? Either way, I'd never forget him.

"Hey, Annie!" Zoe called from the beach. "We're playing a game to see who gets the last cupcake. You want to join?"

I smiled, turning and splashing back toward my friends. "I'm in!"

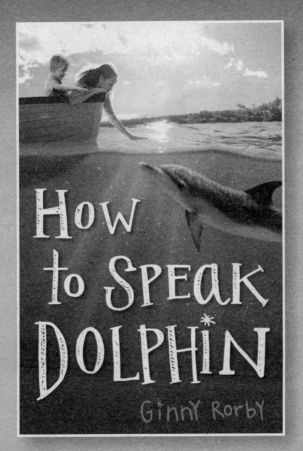

How to SPEAK DOLPHIN

Ginny Rorby

Nori, a captive dolphin, seems like the solution
to all of Lily's family's problems. But Lily sees
that Nori deserves to be free. Can she help the
dolphin without betraying her own family?

■ SCHOLASTIC
scholastic.com

Wendy Mass's birthday books are like a wish come true!

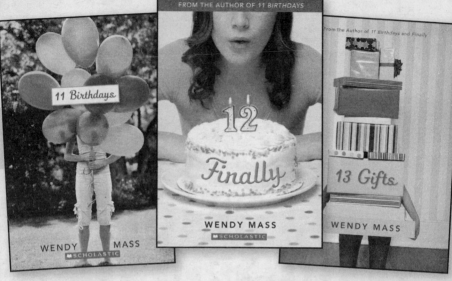